GREEK MYTHS:
Gods, Heroes and Monsters

Books by Ellen Switzer

There Ought to Be a Law
How Democracy Failed
Our Urban Planet
Dancers!: Horizons in American Dance
The Nutcracker
Greek Myths: Gods, Heroes and Monsters

Greek Myths: Gods, Heroes and Monsters

Their Sources, Their Stories and

Their Meanings

by ELLEN SWITZER

and COSTAS

with photographs by COSTAS

A Jean Karl Book

ATHENEUM · 1988 · New York

To Jean Karl

Our favorite editor and good friend

—ELLEN SWITZER & COSTAS

Text copyright © 1988 by Ellen Switzer and Costas
Photographs copyright © 1988 by Costas

Atheneum
Macmillan Publishing Company
866 Third Avenue, New York, NY 10022
Collier Macmillan Canada, Inc.

Type set by Arcata Graphics/Kingsport, Kingsport, Tennessee
Printed and bound by Fairfield Graphics, Fairfield, Pennsylvania
Designed by Mary Ahern
First Edition
3 5 7 9 11 13 15 17 19 20 18 16 14 12 10 8 6 4 2
Library of Congress Cataloging-in-Publication Data

Switzer, Ellen Eichenwald.
Greek Myths: Gods, Heroes and Monsters: Their Sources, Their Stories and
Their Meanings/by Ellen Switzer;
photographs by Costas.—1st ed. p. cm.
SUMMARY: Examines the sources and stories of Greek mythology,
recounting the tales of gods, heroes, lovers, and warriors.
ISBN 0–689–31253–9
1. Mythology, Greek—Juvenile literature. [1. Mythology, Greek.]
I. Costas. II. Costas, ill. III. Title.
BL782.S93 1988   292′.13—dc19
87–22690 CIP AC

CONTENTS

Part Four
GREAT HEROES AND HEROINES

Part Five
POPULAR LEGENDS AND FAIRY TALES

Part Six
THE TROJAN WAR

Part Seven
AFTER THE TROJAN WAR

PREFACE

Everywhere in the world, wherever groups of people built settlements that grew into villages, cities, or countries, they told and retold stories to explain events they could not understand: Where did thunder and lightning come from? Why did one year produce a good harvest and another a disastrous one? Why did bad things happen to good people? What happened to the human spirit after death?

Also, for entertainment and inspiration, they invented heroes and heroines who accomplished deeds of which they themselves could only dream. These stories were passed along from generation to generation, and became a body of commonly held beliefs. As such, they made up the mythology of peoples who shared common customs and language.

Greek mythology is unique in that it is so totally earthbound. In today's Greece, any tourist who asks the right questions will be shown the cave (though some say it was a hut) where Odysseus hid before entering Ithaca, the spot where the priestess of Apollo pronounced the oracles, the hill on which Agamemnon's palace stood, with the overhang on which Clytemnestra waited for the husband she planned to murder. Occasionally someone will even explain exactly which mountaintop in the Atlas range is Olympus. And when I visited these sites, searching for the sources of myth, it seemed somehow as if the ghosts of the gods who lived there still walked.

Costas, who photographed all the pictures for this book, was born and brought up on the island that, supposedly, was Homer's home. On Chios, more than anywhere else, the spirits of the Greek gods and heroes seem to become part of the atmosphere of everyday life, to share the same space with today's generation.

For this book, Costas not only worked as a photographer, taking pictures of the places where the gods and heroes supposedly performed their magical deeds, but also acted as a collaborator, helping collect some of the lesser-known versions of the stories we included.

There are few "official" versions of Greek myths. Often they change, depending on who is telling them. And, as they continue to be told today, they keep changing. Costas knows, from his own childhood, versions of stories that people from other places do not know.

At Delphi and Corfu we found inveterate storytellers who enjoyed giving the local version of whatever myth we were researching at the moment. Most of those people spoke only Greek, and Costas served as a translator as well as someone who would occasionally argue the virtues and vices of a particular god or hero, in much the same way as he might discuss some of today's political leaders, writers, or other celebrities.

So this book is a true collaboration. Without Costas's knowledge of the country of his birth and its atmosphere and mythology, I could not have written the stories in the many shades of colors that reflect their folk origins. And no photographer who did not half believe that somehow, somewhere, many of these heroic beings existed could have taken the special photographs in this book. They give the rest of us an impression of the mysterious, occasionally eerie, sometimes evil, spirit that pervades the places the ancient Greeks considered holy.

Ellen Switzer

INTRODUCTION

The Greeks created their gods and goddesses in their own image. Theirs was an earth- and nature-bound religion, with the world as they knew it at the center of their universe, and the men and women whom they knew and understood at the center of that world. In many of the myths, the gods walked among the people, often not even recognized as divine beings. Not only were they human in appearance, but also in character, moral values, and behavior.

There were beautiful gods and a few ugly ones. Gods could, on occasion, be generous, fair, and reasonable, but just as frequently they were petty, jealous, vain, and inconsistent. Even though they had superhuman strength—they could destroy mere humans with lightning, thunderbolts, and floods, if provoked—they could themselves be hurt by other gods. They were certainly not omnipotent, nor did they necessarily know what the future held for *them*, although they could foretell the future of their human subjects. Zeus, the chief of the gods, was frequently warned by other gods that "fate" had power even over him, and that, if he tried to interfere with the workings of that unknown and unknowable power, he might come to a bad end.

The temples the Greeks built and the sacrifices they made to their gods were not really acts of worship. Actually, by today's standards they might well be regarded as a form of bribery, or a payment for services rendered. When the Greek gods did not get the material awards they expected, they could get downright nasty. So, religious observances became acts of appeasement.

And, as one reads or listens to the stories about the gods, they are not beings in whom anyone could have much trust. They were too unpredictable, and often behaved from motives that were too selfish to be counted upon for justice. When a just man suffered, an unjust god might be angry or have succumbed to an attack of bad temper.

When not busy among the earthlings, the gods lived, not in some distant heaven, but right in the middle of Greece, in a real, visible place. Their home was Mount Olympus, probably an ancient name for the highest peak in the Atlas mountain range. The top of the mountain was frequently shrouded in mist or clouds, which allowed the gods to conduct their private lives without being constantly observed by prying human eyes. They may have felt they needed that privacy to hide some of their less than godly behavior from each other as well as from humanity.

But in spite of this cloud cover, the Greeks told many highly unflattering stories about those godly private lives, much as today's gossip columnnists write about the current crop of the rich and famous. Zeus's love affairs and Hera's constant jealousy made for many amusing tales. Aphrodite was the goddess of love and beauty, but her deceptions of her ugly and lame but decent and hardworking husband, Hephaestus, the god of the forge, made her seem more like a vain flirt than a divine being. Hermes, with wings on his feet, was beautiful, athletic, and clever. His father, Zeus, often used him as a messenger. But he was also downright dishonest. Even Athena, the goddess of wisdom and the protector of the city of Athens (named after her), could let hurt pride rather than justice guide her behavior.

Because the gods and goddesses did not set a perfect example for human behavior, they also provided no universal standards of morality. There are no Ten Commandments in Greek mythology. There were no religious preachers either. Priests made the sacrifices that the gods expected in return for their favors. Morality was left to philosophers.

If the gods and goddesses had very human flaws, so did mythical heroes (there were very few heroines in Greek legend). Although a man had to be physically beautiful, strong, and brave to be considered a genuine hero, he could be (and often was) deceitful, dishonest, and cruel. If Zeus could repeatedly deceive his wife, so could the heroes of Greek legend, who constantly betrayed the women who loved them. Sometimes those women exacted a terrible revenge. Often they just suffered silently.

There are few moral judgments in these stories. Greek men and women apparently did not expect to be judged for their virtues in their life on earth, and they did not expect reward or punishment in the afterlife either.

According to most Greek mythology, humans who died went to a land called Hades, ruled by a god of the same name. Hades, unlike Mount Olympus, was not a visible place. It was somewhere over the edge of the visible world, deep inside the earth, and could be entered only through one of several hidden entrances, through deep caverns and mysterious lakes. In that darkness was the river Styx, which the newly dead had to cross to get to their final home.

Hades was a world inhabited by shadows. According to early legends, the ghosts of all the dead in Hades floated about as if they were in some miserable dream. No matter how good or bad their behavior had been on earth, in Hades everyone was equal.

Later legends do provide special punishments for those who entered Hades after committing some particularly heinous sins during their life on earth. For instance, there was Tantalus, a son of Zeus and a mortal woman. The gods honored him beyond all of the other mortal children of Zeus. They even let him eat at their table on Olympus. But Tantalus was jealous of the gods instead of grateful. To dishonor them, he invited them to his own home for dinner, killed his son (Zeus's grandson), Pelops, and cooked him to serve as the main meal. Of course, the Olympians realized immediately what he had done. They decided to punish him as no man had ever been punished before to prevent such an outrage from occurring again. They killed him and set him in a pool in Hades, where he was forever condemned to tormenting thirst and hunger. Whenever he stooped to drink from the pool's waters, they disappeared, only to reappear as soon as he stood upright again. Above his head grew the most delicious fruits the gods could devise, but whenever he stretched up to pick one to eat, a wind would blow the branch out of his reach. Thus he stood forever, his undying thirst never quenched, his hunger never appeased.

Then there are the Danaids. They were fifty young women who, for some reason the legend does not explain, were totally opposed to marriage. When they were married off against their will, they killed their husbands. For that sin they were condemned to spend eternity carrying water from the river Styx in leaking jars.

Occasionally, someone who seemed relatively innocent was also condemned to extra horror in Hades. There was Sisyphus, whose main sin seems to have been that he suspected Zeus of turning himself into an eagle and carrying off his beautiful daughter. Since Zeus did this kind of thing many times, the suspicion was not entirely unjustified, but Zeus took offense anyhow, and poor Sisyphus was condemned to spend eternity in Hades trying to roll a large rock up a hill, and having it forever roll back down on him. His punishment was almost as terrible as that endured by the child-murderer Tantalus, but his sin was, at worst, a mistake. So even in Hades, justice apparently did not always prevail when it came to dealing out extra punishments.

Still later legends do refer to an alternate afterlife, where a few of the select were allowed to spend eternity: the Elysian Fields, a place filled with joy, music, light, and pleasure. But those who were assigned to the Elysian Fields instead of Hades did not get there by real merit. Goodness and mercy, honesty, and faithfulness counted for very little. Those who were granted a passport to the Elysian Fields were either highly accomplished artistically or especially beautiful physically, and therefore pleasing to some particular god. According to some legends, Helen of Troy, the woman who left her husband to run away with her lover (and thus caused all the misery of the Trojan War), spent her afterlife in the Elysian Fields. She escaped the misery of Hades, while other much more virtuous women did not.

There was only one character flaw, the Greeks thought, that the gods would never forgive. The Greek word for that particular sin is *hubris.* It translates loosely as "wanton arrogance, resulting in excessive pride." It usually consisted of the belief of specific individuals that they could accomplish anything, or were, in some way, untouchable. Often persons with hubris felt that they had been singled out in some special way from their fellows. Hubris always led to death in the case of humans, and banishment in the case of gods.

So Greek gods and heroes were flawed. But it is those very flaws, which made them all so human, that permitted them to survive the civilization that created them. Greek gods and goddesses are still among us, in our drama, novels, and poetry, our music, art, and dance. The father of modern psychiatry, Sigmund Freud, used figures in Greek mythology as symbols in his own system of analyzing and classifying the behavior of his patients in twentieth-century Vienna. When he wrote about the "Oedipus complex," he knew that his fellow scientists would know exactly who Oedipus was—the Greek hero who had killed his father and married his mother (see Chapter 24).

Egyptian gods, who usually were strange combinations of humans and animals, did not survive in a similar way because it was impossible for the men and women of later ages to identify with them.

The Nordic gods probably did not survive in the arts because, although they looked like human beings, they did not behave like them. They were either all good or all bad, without that mix of virtue and vice to make them interesting. Richard Wagner seems to have been the only recent artist committed to retelling their stories, and he had to make up a lot of new material to keep them more up-to-date. He wrote a series of operas about Nordic gods and heroes, but even with all the new and more modern touches added by the composer, they somehow don't translate into our own lives and times as the Greeks do.

Wotan, the chief Germanic god, had his thunder and lightning bolts to toss about, but unlike Zeus, he did not have all those earthly love affairs. There was no god who combined thievery and a good sense of business like Mercury. Fricka, the wife of Wotan and the goddess of home and hearth, and Freya, the goddess of love and beauty, seem like rather stolid German housewives, spending most of their time weaving and spinning. Neither would have dared to nag Wotan, who ruled the roost much more effectively, and much less interestingly, than Zeus.

Greek legends give us a good picture of the life the Greeks lived in the days that the stories were told. But since many of the stories were told and retold long before a written language was available, they changed from time to time and from place to place, depending on the teller.

As inevitably happens when stories are preserved by word of mouth, they are not always consistent. Apparently at different times and in different places, different versions of stories about the gods and goddesses and heroes were told. In some parts of Greece, a tragic story acquired an unexpected happy ending. To try to track down the various sources of these different versions is not possible, of course. Perhaps, in one place, the most gifted storyteller was a pessimist, while in another he was the kind of optimist who liked to leave his listeners in a good mood by allowing a hero to live instead of sending him to his death, or even by allowing him to go to the Elysian Fields when, in every other version of the legend, he went straight to Hades.

Also, because the stories are so clearly rooted in human experience, as the stories changed, one can also guess at how life-styles and, perhaps, values changed. We get to know the ancient Greeks as people, not statues or paintings, through the stories they told, because the characters in those stories behave so much like men and women behave today. We recognize *ourselves* in the myths and legends, and can identify with Greek civilization through those very human gods and heroes.

The Romans, who conquered the Greeks, eventually borrowed the Greek gods for themselves, but gave them different names. Occasionally they also changed an individual god's character to fit their own customs and ideas. In Rome the gods had temples, which were essentially public places, and festivals, which were considered holidays for the common folk.

The Romans also had a habit of creating new gods at certain

times—usually emperors or empresses who had recently died. Becoming a god usually had very little to do with these rulers' virtue, and a great deal to do with their offspring's political power. Having a father or a mother who had been made a god tended to lessen the possibility of revolution for the surviving son or daughter. Of course, while alive, a ruler also aspired to become a god. It was considered an honor, rather like a baseball player who is entered in the Hall of Fame.

The Greeks were never very interested in whether or not the inhabitants of other countries were loyal to the Greek religion, since they themselves did not take it very seriously. The Romans considered their religion a political fact of life. A foreign country that they had conquered was required to observe the Roman religion mainly as a way of affirming Roman civil authority. Romans regarded non-Romans who did not swear loyalty to the gods as potential traitors who might also be disloyal to the Roman state. To prevent this possibility, they frequently executed religious dissenters, including all the Christians they threw to the lions in the Roman Colosseum.

Since much of Greek myth and legend was not written down until centuries after it was first created, we can assume that many stories have been lost to us. But we may also presume that those stories that the Greeks loved best—those that they told most often and continued to tell—have survived from the preliterate age.

In this book we tell some of those stories again, sometimes in more than one version.

They allow us to know a great deal about an ancient civilization, about the men and women who lived then: their ideas, their customs, their joys, and their suffering. They let us know that over the centuries much about what makes us all human has changed very little. After all, it is those stories that make the ancient Greeks come alive. The beautiful marble statues and temples they left behind show us what kinds of artists they were. The myths and legends show us what kinds of *people* walked, talked, loved, lived, and died in those long-ago times.

PART ONE

The Earliest Stories

Chapter 1

Those Who Told the Myths and Legends First

Greek myths and legends, like all folktales, represent one of the ways by which our long-ago ancestors tried to explain the workings of the universe and the fortunes and misfortunes in their own lives.

Thousands of years ago, men and women looked at the world around them and tried to make sense of it. What caused the seasons to change? Why were there storms, floods, volcanic eruptions? What caused some years to produce good harvests and others killing frosts, not enough rain, or mysterious plant diseases that killed off the grain and fruit?

All of us seem to have an inborn need to try to make sense of the world around us and of our own lives. Throughout human history, myths and legends have been one way we have tried. Science has been another. The Greeks used both. Through science they tried to find methods of changing their lives for the better. Through myth and legend they explained what they thought they could not change.

The earliest clues as to who first told the Greek legends and myths and what these myths and legends were are found on very ancient art objects that have been unearthed by archaeologists. There are pieces of painted pottery, fragments of sculpture, ruins of temples that go back many thousands of years. These ancient Greeks were superb artists and craftsmen as well as fine storytellers.

Obviously, the isolated archaeological fragments that have been found don't tell whole stories. But, in hindsight, they confirm the fact that many of the tales later poets and dramatists wrote down had existed for many generations. From the artistic fragments, we know that the early Athena wore a helmet and carried a spear, that Hermes had wings on his feet and his helmet, that Hercules fought many fearsome beasts, and that Odysseus, or someone like him, sailed the seas.

The first generally accepted versions of much of Greek legend and myth appear in the *Iliad* and the *Odyssey*, which, by common consent, mark the very beginnings of European literature. However, contrary to what many people believe, even those two great master-pieces probably were not originally written down.

In those long-ago centuries, outstanding storytellers wandered from town to town, practicing their art before local audiences, gathered in public squares or theaters. Those who attended probably repeated the stories they heard to their children and grandchildren, and so much of ancient Greek myth was kept alive through the centuries.

HOMER

Most scholars now believe that sometime before 750 B.C. (some say as early as 1000 B.C.), there lived one particularly outstanding wandering minstrel whose talents were greater than those of any of the previous storytellers. He told his tales all over Greece, and probably was considered a kind of celebrity. We know very little about this man, but many experts believe that he was probably called Homer. Many cities and towns claim him, but one of the strongest claims is put forth by the Greek island of Chios, near the coast of Turkey, where the city of Troy (which may or may not have been fictitious) was located.

Those are all the facts we know about Homer. All the stories about his blindness, his limp, the laurel wreaths around his head, et cetera, did not originate in ancient Greece. They first appeared some time around the fifteenth century in Europe, and became very popular in the nineteenth century, when ancient Greece in general and poetry in particular enjoyed great popularity.

It is not an accident that several encyclopedias, which carefully check the accuracy of their entries, contain only a few paragraphs about the poet Homer. In one, the city of Homer, Indiana, gets at least four times as much space. Obviously, we *know* a lot more about Homer, Indiana, than we do about the poet Homer.

Most scholars assume that Homer did not *write* either the *Iliad* or the *Odyssey*, simply because at the time that this poet must have lived the Greeks as yet had no alphabet, no written language. Experts assume that his stories were preserved because he had a group of followers who learned the legends from him—possibly word for word—and passed them along to later generations.

How do we know that the *Iliad* and the *Odyssey* were the work of *one poet*? Actually, we don't. Indeed, there are some scholars who believe that Homer is a collective name for several of the minstrels who wandered across Greece sometime around 800 B.C. But most experts now feel that there had to be *one main poet*, simply because the style of the work is so consistent. There are images that keep appearing and reappearing. Adjectives used to describe landscapes, gods and goddesses, heroes and villains are similar throughout the works.

What's more, there is another element, not quite so obvious but nonetheless convincing, that makes experts in ancient literature believe that one mind was responsible for at least the core of these two magnificent stories. Certain ideas of good and evil, honor and dishonor—the qualities that distinguish a hero from an ordinary mortal—are present throughout the two epic poems. We know that what one person may consider admirable, another person may not, even if both lived at the same time in the same culture. What one writer may consider an unforgivable sin, another may simply think of as a human error. The philosophy and outlook that is evident throughout the *Iliad* and the *Odyssey* seems to represent the point of view of one individual. For instance, throughout the *Iliad* and the *Odyssey*, Helen of Troy, the woman who, according to legend, was a faithless, vain woman, responsible for the whole tragedy of the Trojan War, is not regarded as a villainous person. The author of the two epics looked upon her as a woman whose incomparable beauty (for which she was not responsible) seduced both men and gods. She had little or no free will to stop the events she caused, and therefore was not punished. Indeed, the Greeks, including her husband, Menelaus, took no revenge on her. Even after all the years she had lived in Troy with her lover, Paris (who was killed), Menelaus took her back. He seemed to have been won over by her beauty almost immediately, and took her home with him, where, presumably, they lived as happily as Greeks in epics ever do.

The much more admirable women of Troy were either killed or taken away as slaves by the conquerors. The most admirable Trojan woman of all, Andromache, the widow of Hector (see Chapter 30), was not only taken off to slavery, but her infant son was torn from her arms and she watched him being thrown from the walls of Troy to his death. In Homer's world, the gods did not rule justly; terrible events happened to good and bad people alike.

There is a slight change of emphasis in the *Odyssey*. For instance, fierce warriors, no matter how cruel, are considered heroes in the *Iliad*. To be a "sacker of cities" (i.e., a general who burned a city down, murdered most of the male population, and took women and children as slaves) is to be considered a good warrior and, therefore, a hero. In the *Odyssey*, "sackers of cities" are looked upon with considerably less sympathy, and there is some real pity for their victims. But if the outlook and philosophy of the *Iliad* and the *Odyssey* differed this way, why do most scholars still believe that both works originated with the same poet? There are the similarities in style, in the way people are described, and the words used to evoke a certain atmosphere of mystery that seem unique and, therefore, probably the words of one man. What could have happened is that the *Odyssey*, which is really a sequel to the *Iliad*, may have been composed when the poet was much older, and his own values and outlook had changed. This happens to many people now and probably happened in ancient Greece as well.

H E S I O D

Hesiod is the first *writer* of legends and myths for whom we have any positive biographical information. He probably lived sometime in late eighth or early seventh century B.C., at a time when a written language had come into use. Fragments of his writings exist. Some call him the father of written Greek poetry.

Experts assume that Hesiod and his brother, Peres, were born at Ascra, near Mount Helicon. At any rate, Hesiod refers to this location as the place where he grew up and tended his father's flocks.

According to his own story, he received a commission directly from the Muses (the divine spirits of the arts) to be their prophet and poet. He set to work to write songs and poems in praise of the gods and heroes of early Greece, and won several poetry contests, which apparently were part of the entertainment at the athletic games held regularly in Greece in those days.

Much of Hesiod's poetry had to do with quarrels within his own family, as well as his own daily life and work. But in one of the works attributed to him, *Theogony*, there are many myths and legends that appear in the works of well-known Greek dramatists and Roman poets.

Hesiod, apparently, was a rather methodical, humorless man, much given to self-glorification, who delighted in giving advice on everything from how to grow the best wheat to how to deal with one's wayward brother. His work lacks the genius that is so apparent in the *Iliad* and the *Odyssey*, in the works of the Greek dramatists, and in the Roman poets. His fame rests on the fact that some of his stories and ideas were in *writing* and served as source material for later, more gifted authors.

A P O L L O N I U S   O F   R H O D E S

The works of this poet, who lived about four hundred years after Hesiod, were mostly destroyed in the tragic fires that burned down the libraries in Alexandria and Constantinople. But the early Roman poets Virgil and Ovid refer to him as one of their principal sources for some of the legends and myths they incorporated in their works.

THE GREEK THEATER

Although the Greek plays were first written and performed several hundred years after the myths and legends were first written down, they may be our best sources today for the stories they tell.

The first presentation of what might be called a play took place in Athens in 534 B.C., as part of a contest of poets held annually as a religious ceremony. Those poets who produced the most interesting descriptions or the most dramatic retellings of well-known tales won the prizes, but changes in the basic storyline of a legend or in the characterization of a god or a hero were not allowed.

However, in 534 B.C., one of the poet contestants, whose name was Thespis, made a drastic change in *form*, not content, of one of the legends. Instead of reciting his poem, he acted it out, impersonating each character with a difference in voice and expression. The audience apparently loved the innovation, and he won the coveted prize, though some of the political and artistic leaders of his time accused him of changing Greek tradition and turning a religious ritual into mere entertainment.

His popularity overcame the objections, however, and within a few years the recitations had turned into real plays instead of just one-man shows. Different actors represented different characters. They were all men; no women were allowed to participate in these religious ceremonies. Female parts were played by young men with high voices. All actors wore masks, so they could not be recognized as individuals. After all, each represented a religious figure, who was not to be confused with the contemporary human person who portrayed him or her.

In the years that followed, there were probably hundreds of different plays and dozens of playwrights, but only a small number of these have come down to us. We know from them that the plays followed certain rigid principles. No violence was ever shown onstage, for instance. Although Greek myths and legends tend to be full of murder, mayhem, and rape, audiences learned about these events only from conversations between the characters onstage or commentary from the chorus.

A play rarely presented a whole legend from beginning to end. Usually, the playwright took one part of a legend and expanded on it. Presumably the Greeks who saw the play would know the whole tale. The plays are also singularly nonjudgmental. Some of the characters commit terrible deeds: Medea kills her children to avenge herself on her unfaithful husband; Clytemnestra kills her husband; and her son, Orestes, kills her in turn. But in almost all the plays, the killers are not portrayed as unmitigated sinners. There are usually circumstances that make their deeds understandable, if not necessarily excusable. And all characters are, to a certain extent, at the mercy of the gods, who themselves may be ruled by an overpowering fate.

Of the innumerable Greek poets and authors who wrote plays, three were most honored in their own time. It is evident that the Greeks had excellent literary and artistic judgment, for the same three playwrights are still considered to be among the greatest dramatists of all time. They are Aeschylus (525 B.C.–456 B.C.), Sophocles (496 B.C.–406 B.C.), and Euripides (485 B.C.–406 B.C.).

Although much of the work of these three great dramatists is lost, enough of it remains to show us in vivid characterization and poetic language what masterpieces they managed to create. They did this in spite of a system of censorship, and within the boundaries of form and content dictated by the religious nature of theatrical performances. The works of all three playwrights are still performed throughout the world, translated into dozens of languages. One of the most astounding performances of Euripides' *Medea* electrified audiences in New York City's Central Park a few summers ago. Although it was presented in Japanese, members of the audience wept and screamed as the distraught heroine's nurse told of the murder of Medea's two children.

It is probably these plays that have kept Greek myths and legends almost as alive to us today as to the audiences in the Greek theaters who watched them almost twenty-five hundred years ago.

Chapter 2

How the World Began:

The Greek Version

SOURCES: The very early creation legends are difficult to trace to their original sources, since they were passed along by word of mouth from one generation to the next. There are many different legends about the origin of the earth, some similar to those told in other primitive cultures. It is interesting that in almost all of these legends the originating power is *female,* and that often she creates what later becomes the earth and its people without the assistance of a male being.

For us, the stories about Zeus and his family of gods and goddesses have many different sources, including Homer, Hesiod, Apollonius of Rhodes, and the major Greek dramatists. In addition, some of the details about the Greek divinities now appear only in the writings of the Roman poets Ovid and Virgil. These two later writers tell the stories as if they had heard or read about them somewhere else, perhaps in older works that are lost to us.

THE STORY: According to one of the earliest stories, Eurynome, the goddess of all things, rose naked from *Chaos* (a Greek word meaning something like "complete disorder") but found nothing for her feet to stand on. Therefore, she divided the sea from the sky, but there still was no place where she could rest. So, to warm herself, she danced upon the waves to the south, and winds followed her. She caught the north wind, which in her hands turned into a huge serpent. The serpent coiled around her, and she became pregnant.

Next she assumed the form of a great dove and laid a huge egg, which the serpent kept warm until it hatched. The egg brought forth all the things that now exist: the sun, the moon, the planets, the stars, and the earth with its mountains and valleys, streams and lakes, and all its living creatures, including, presumably, the first humans.

Eurynome and the serpent made their home on Mount Olympus, but, like many of the later gods, they soon quarreled. Apparently the serpent made Eurynome angry because he claimed that *he*, not she, was actually the author of the universe. So she banished him from Mount Olympus to a dark cave, miles below the earth.

She then created seven planetary powers, each with a god and a goddess as rulers, among them Cronus and Rhea, who ruled the earth. They became the parents of Zeus. Later Zeus and other members of his family banished or killed Cronus and Rhea, depending on which myth you read.

In another version of the creation, Mother Earth emerged from *Chaos* and gave birth to her son, Uranus. His son, Cronus, became king of the gods when he killed his father, and was then himself killed or banished by his son, Zeus.

According to one myth, Cronus was warned of his fate by his dying father, Uranus, who told him that "evil will beget only evil. If you murder me and steal my throne, one of your own sons will murder *you* in turn."

So Cronus was very careful. One by one he swallowed all his children right after they were born: first three daughters, Hestia, Demeter, and Hera; and then two sons, Hades and Poseidon.

His wife, Rhea, was, of course, furious. She schemed to make sure that her husband would not swallow their next child. After she gave birth to another son, whom she named Zeus, she hid him in a cradle in the branches of an olive tree. Then she found a rock, wrapped it in a blanket, and held it to her breast.

When Cronus saw her with what he thought was yet another

baby, he did not even bother to check. He swallowed the stone, blanket and all.

Then Rhea prepared a special drink, which made Cronus sick. The next morning he vomited up first the stone, and then all the sons and daughters he had swallowed. Meanwhile, Zeus was growing up to be a beautiful young god. He and his brothers and sisters banded together to dethrone their cruel father, and started the war that was to make Zeus and some of his brothers and sisters the rulers of the universe.

Chapter 3

The War of the Gods

As Zeus was growing up and turning from a baby into a beautiful young boy, Rhea continued to hide him. She realized he would need care, and so she gave him to a shepherd to raise, promising that in return for good treatment of her son, she would make sure that none of his sheep would ever be eaten by wolves.

When Zeus had become a man, Cronus still did not know of his existence, and Rhea was able to introduce him into the Olympian court as a cupbearer to his father. According to some legends, he actually was the person who mixed the potion that induced Cronus to vomit up all of his brothers and sisters.

At any rate, the young gods, now newly arrived on Olympus, were exceedingly grateful to their brother for delivering them from their father's stomach, and they elected him as their leader. They planned to overthrow Cronus, and their mother, Rhea, agreed to help them.

Cronus had always been guarded by a race of Titans, who were his half-brothers. They were huge warriors, who were led by the tallest and strongest Titan of them all: Atlas.

Early in his reign, Cronus had banished two other monster races deep in the bowels of the earth, locked away forever, he thought, from sunlight and power. They were the Cyclops, who were exceedingly ugly but very clever. Each had only one eye, placed in the middle of his forehead. Also locked up were the creatures the Greeks called the Hundred-Headed Ones. They, too, were very ugly, which was one of the reasons they had been banished from Olympus. Like almost all gods of ancient Greece, Cronus loved beauty and wanted only beautiful creatures around him. However, the Hundred-Headed Ones were not only strong, but also exceedingly difficult to kill. Apparently, if just one head survived a battle, the individual would go on living.

Rhea helped Zeus and his brothers and sisters find the keys to the door, deep inside the earth, that locked up all the monsters who, naturally enough, hated Cronus for banishing them. Zeus formed them into an army, which he led against his father and the Titans.

At first it seemed as if the mighty Titans were unbeatable, but the clever Cyclops had hidden some weapons that they gave to Zeus and his brothers. Zeus got a thunderbolt. Hades was given a helmet that made him invisible, and Poseidon got a trident, a weapon with three sharp points at the top.

With these new weapons, the young gods gained an advantage. Hades was able to sneak into Cronus's presence and open the doors to his chambers without being seen. Poseidon threatened his father with his trident, and so distracted him from watching Zeus, who killed him with the thunderbolt.

The Titans fought back courageously, but without a leader they were at a disadvantage. Zeus and his army drove them down from Mount Olympus. The Titans attacked fiercely every step of the way. As soon as the young gods thought they had won, a new troop of Titans would join the battle. The war lasted for more than one hundred years, and during that time the earth was in constant turmoil, with storms, hurricanes, earthquakes, and erupting volcanos threatening all humans and animals, who cowered in caves to escape the wrath of the fighting gods.

When Zeus saw that his allies, the Cyclops, were growing tired, he called in his reserve troops, the Hundred-Headed Ones, whom he had hidden in ambush. They took up huge boulders and hurled them down at the Titans. The Titans thought that Mount Olympus was collapsing under their feet, and they broke ranks and fled.

The young god Pan, who was related to Zeus, gave such a shout of joy that he frightened the Titans even more. Their defeat became a rout. Pan always could shout loud enough to scare both enemies and friends. (That is where we get the word "panic," incidentally.)

The young gods were now clearly the victors. They climbed to the top of Mount Olympus, took over the castle, and elected Zeus as their king. No one is sure what happened to the Titans. According to some legends, they were killed by the victorious armies. According to other legends, they were banished deep into the bowels of the earth, where they occasionally still cause trouble in the form of earthquakes and volcanic eruptions.

Atlas was singled out for special punishment. He was condemned to carry the heavens forever on his shoulders. Even though he was strong, this incredible burden was terribly painful, and made it impossible for him to start any kind of revolt against the new rulers.

Rhea, who had helped her son Zeus overthrow his father, was, of course, allowed to remain on Olympus. But she apparently lost much of her importance once her husband, King Cronus, was gone. There are few later myths that even mention her name. So we can assume that she went into some sort of dignified retirement, as the widows of former rulers often do, and allowed her three sons to rule the universe.

The sons—Zeus, Poseidon, and Hades—threw dice to see who would have first choice as to which part of the universe he would rule. Zeus won and chose the sky. Poseidon was second. He was rather pleased that Zeus had chosen the heavens, because they looked so empty. He picked what he would have chosen even if he had won the lottery: the sea. He had always preferred the waters for two reasons: He loved adventures and he loved secrets. The oceans were eminently suitable for both. Poor Hades, who was always unlucky, got what was left, and what nobody wanted: the underworld. The earth was supposed to be held as a neutral area, and originally the goddesses were appointed to manage it. When the gods began to realize how important the earth, with all its human beings, really was, they decided to take charge there jointly. Of course, that made some of the goddesses very angry, but the gods were more powerful and, as usual, got what they wanted.

PART TWO

The Royal Family of Gods

Chapter 4 *Zeus*

SOURCES: Word-of-mouth folktales, pottery fragments, sculptures, and other archaeological finds from the preliterate age, as well as Hesiod, Homer, and some of the early Greek dramatists.

THE STORY: Zeus had been named the king and the father of heaven after he led his brother and sister gods to victory over Cronus. He had also been given the most powerful of the weapons devised by his allies, the Cyclops. With his thunderbolt he was able to control his often rebellious, and usually quarrelsome, family on Olympus. He was able to turn himself into all kinds of beings: human, animal, vegetable, and mineral, and although he rarely was able to use this trick on other gods, who could see through his various disguises, he often fooled human beings, especially women whom he wanted to seduce.

Once he was able to use it on his mother, Rhea. She foresaw that his constant pursuit of women was eventually going to get him into all kinds of trouble, so she forbade him to marry. Zeus, like most human beings, was not able to recognize his own faults. And like other powerful persons, he did not want to take orders, even sensible ones, so he decided to punish his mother. He turned himself into a serpent and almost strangled her. After that, presumably, she kept quiet.

Zeus eventually married his sister Hera, but just as Rhea had prophesied, both lived to regret the marriage. There is almost no evidence in legend and myth that they were happy together even for one day. Zeus was constantly unfaithful to his wife, and, understandably enough, this soured Hera's disposition. She nagged Zeus unmercifully, but, since he could have disposed of her at any time with his thunderbolt, she had little choice but to accept his deceptions. Occasionally she humiliated him by scolding him or making fun of him in front of the other gods. Often she would take terrible vengeance on the women to whom Zeus had made love, their children, and occasionally even their grandchildren. This, of course, was usually very unfair, since most of these women met Zeus when he was in disguise, and therefore had no idea that he was either a god or married. Hera even tortured women whom her husband had carried away by force—an early instance of blaming the victim.

Only once did the royal family decide that Zeus's arrogance and unfairness had become intolerable. Hera, helped by Poseidon and Apollo, concocted a plot to keep Zeus prisoner on Olympus so that he could no longer meddle in the affairs of the rest of the universe. Most of the other gods did not take an active part in the revolt, but agreed that it seemed like a very good idea.

Hera, Poseidon, and Apollo surrounded Zeus while he was asleep on his couch and bound him with rawhide thongs knotted into hundreds of knots, so that he could not move and grab for his thunderbolt to punish them for their insubordination.

When he awoke, he was, of course, furious. He threatened them all with instant death, but since they had removed his weapon, they just laughed at him and adjourned to another room to decide who would take Zeus's place as ruler of Olympus. However, like many revolutionaries who depose dictators, once they had won an apparent victory, they became jealous of one another. Many of the gods and some of the goddesses wanted to be the one in charge of Olympus. While they were quarreling, Nereid, a female Titan who had been spared when Zeus banished all the Titan males, decided that anything would be better than another civil war on Olympus, even Zeus with all his faults. So she untied the knots and released Zeus to wreak vengeance on his disobedient relatives.

Hera received the worst punishment. She was hung from the sky with a golden bracelet on each wrist and an anvil fastened to each ankle. Her co-conspirators were disturbed by her piteous cries, but since Zeus had his thunderbolt back, not one of them had the courage to try to help her. Eventually Zeus freed her himself after extracting a solemn promise that she would never rebel against his authority again.

Poseidon and Apollo were punished by being sent, temporarily, as bond servants to an earthly king, Laomedon, for whom they built the city of Troy. Certainly to be turned from a god into a hardworking slave must have been exceedingly humiliating. Zeus freed the two after he also made them swear not to question his actions in the future.

Besides ruling his divine family, Zeus also kept the stars and the planets in order, made laws (which he often broke himself), enforced oaths, and pronounced oracles. However, like all of the Greek gods, he was not all-powerful. Nothing annoyed him more than being reminded of that fact, which Hera frequently did. Zeus could remember that he had deposed his father, Cronus, and that somehow, somewhere, there was the possibility that the same fate might await him.

Zeus was called Jupiter by the Romans, who made many changes in his character. For the Romans, religion and politics were closely allied. Therefore, having a chief god who chased after women, changed himself into various creatures to accomplish devious purposes, and wandered around the earth instead of ruling his realm from Olympus did not seem appropriate or dignified.

So Zeus became less human and more divine, rather like a super-emperor, who deserved to be treated in literature with the same respect as the Romans' own emperors were supposed to be treated.

The Roman Jupiter, as a result, is much less interesting than the Greek Zeus, and tells us much less about the way the Romans looked at human nature. Their sculptures of Jupiter are much less human, artistic, and interesting than those done by the Greeks. Most Roman Jupiters are fully dressed in some kind of ceremonial clothes with a face that tends to be stiff and rather grim, like the sculptures of obscure local leaders found in squares and parks throughout the Western world.

Chapter 5 *Hera*

Hera is probably the most unpopular of all the Greek divinities. There are almost no legends or myths in which she appears as even reasonably pleasant, never mind kind or generous.

Usually she was up to no good. She tormented those who annoyed her (just about everybody) and was especially wrathful toward those women in whom her husband, Zeus, showed an interest.

The Greeks made sacrifices to her, but one gets the feeling that they did so mainly to keep her from doing them mischief. Even today, Greeks tend to tell their guests that Hera may be responsible for such unpleasant events as ants crawling all over one's picnic, or a wasp stinging one's nose. "Watch out," they are apt to say. "Hera is out to get you."

Of course, Hera had reason for her bitterness and bad temper. Zeus was a terrible husband. Not only was he constantly unfaithful, he often punished Hera if she complained. Nor did the other gods show her much respect.

What's more, she had three thoroughly unpleasant children. Her first son was Ares, the fierce and bloody god of war. Her second was Hephaestus, who was the blacksmith god and forger of weapons. He was probably the kindest of the three, but he was also lame and repulsively ugly. Then there was Eris, her only daughter, the goddess of discord, who loved to ride in Ares' chariot, shrieking at the top of her voice and scaring everybody to death. The rest of Zeus's children, many of whom were not only more powerful, but also much more pleasant, were born out of wedlock.

Hera had one special gift. She could prophesy future events herself, and she could bestow the gift of prophecy on others, gods and humans. However, she usually made sure that the individuals to whom she gave the power to prophesy the future had nothing but disaster to foretell. That, of course, made these men and women very unpopular wherever they went, since nobody likes a gloomy prophet who talks only of sickness, failure, doomed love, and death. So, even Hera's gift was not really a present to enjoy, but a curse to fear.

Just as Zeus—turned into Jupiter in Roman mythology—became a much more respectable and less interesting figure, so did Hera, who was renamed Juno and became a correct Roman matron.

Some Roman empresses had enormous power, and obviously did not enjoy the idea of the wife of the supreme ruler of the universe being a jealous, mean, and frequently rather stupid female. So Juno became more like an idealized empress, walking several steps behind her lord and master, Jupiter, but with a dignity and pride that the Greek Hera rarely displayed. Indeed, Juno's qualities as the lady of the Olympian manor, keeping peace in the family and seeing to it that all the gods were well fed, comfortable, and clean, make her seem more like a perfect housewife than the unsympathetic, nagging Greek mistress of Olympus.

Chapter 6 *Athena*

According to one early legend, Athena was the daughter of Zeus and a Titan maiden, Metis. Zeus, who seems to have had a special liking for tall women, saw Metis, the daughter of his old enemies, walking in a meadow, and started to pursue her.

She turned herself into a hawk to get away, but Zeus turned himself into an even swifter hawk and caught up with her. She flew over the ocean and turned herself into a fish, thinking that no bird would be able to catch her there. But Zeus outsmarted her again. He turned himself into a bigger, stronger fish. Finally, Metis turned herself into a snake, because she knew that Zeus was not fond of snakes, and because as a fish he would not be able to crawl after her on land. But by this time Zeus did not wish to be defeated by a mere woman, even if she was a giantess, so he also turned himself into a snake, and this time she was not able to get away.

Metis became pregnant, and Zeus was rather pleased. But blowing on the winds, he heard a voice that said, "Metis will bear a girl. But, if she gets pregnant again, she will have a son who will depose you as you deposed Cronus."

Zeus, who feared nothing more than that the fates would punish him for what he had done to his own father, decided that Metis had to be destroyed. He found her and swallowed her and her unborn child.

Within an hour he began to feel the worst headache that any being, divine or human, had ever suffered. It seemed to him that there was something inside his skull that was ready to burst out. He also felt sharp pains, as if a spear were thrusting at his brains. He ran to Hephaestus's forge and put his head on the anvil. "Please try to get whatever is inside my head out as quickly as possible," he begged. Hephaestus was frightened, of course. But his father's pain was so terrible that he finally used a sharp sword and split open his head. As soon as he had done so, a tall maiden in full armor, with a sharp spear, leaped out and greeted her father. Zeus's head immediately healed, since, after all, he was a god. He was delighted to see his new daughter.

Because of the way she had been born, springing full-grown from his head, Zeus entrusted Athena with intellectual activities. She invented geometry and the science of the stars. She also, according to some legends, made the first ax, plow, and ox yoke. Her specialty was military strategy, which she enjoyed figuring out like a game. She hated war, however, and her least favorite relative was her half-brother Ares, the god of war.

Generally she was very popular among the other gods, but spent little time with the goddesses, who evidently bored her. She took some time out to teach Hera to spin and weave, however. Hera disliked and feared Athena less than she did most other women, since she looked and acted so much like a man.

Athena became the patron goddess of Athens, where the citizens built many temples for her. She was considered less capricious than the other gods, and generally could be counted on to mete out justice rather than act from whim or spite. But occasionally even she evinced vanity and jealousy. She turned a young woman, Arachne, who had boasted that she was the best weaver in the universe, into a spider. Perhaps she considered Arachne's boast a form of hubris.

Later legends leave out the story of Athena's birth from Zeus's head. She just appeared somehow on a meadow, and was nursed by three nymphs. When she was a very young girl, she accidentally killed a playmate called Pallas in a mock battle, and eventually took her dead friend's name as part of her own, so that in some stories she is known as Pallas Athena.

The Romans called Athena Minerva. Obviously, they did not want an important goddess to be named after a foreign city, especially a city that they eventually conquered.

The Romans were also very much interested in law, and were among the first people to write down laws regarding almost all aspects of life; they elevated lawyers to high positions in government. In Roman sculptures, Minerva is often seen carrying the scales of justice, right along with her shield and spear.

Chapter 7

Apollo and Artemis:

The Twins

A P O L L O

One day Zeus saw a beautiful nymph called Leto and fell in love with her. But he noticed that Hera was watching, and so he changed

Leto and himself into quails, birds that are brown and speckled and can easily hide in trees and bushes. But Hera was too clever for him. She saw through this disguise immediately and put a curse on Leto. She told the unfortunate nymph that she would be pregnant, and that she would not be able to give birth to her child anywhere the sun could shine.

Then she sent the great serpent Python to enforce her curse, to drive Leto from any sunlit spot. Zeus tried to help the mother of his child and sent the south wind to float her to an island called Delos. It was a small, rocky place, but Python followed anyway. However, because the island was so small, the wind could push it farther out to sea faster than the serpent could swim. And so, finally, Leto had a place where she could give birth.

It turned out that she bore twins. First she had a lovely baby girl she called Artemis. From all the running and hiding, she was so weak that she had difficulty giving birth to her second child. But Artemis, even though she was just a baby, helped her mother, and a beautiful son was born. Leto called him Apollo.

Zeus had a great many children, but none he loved so much as those twins. They were gifted with strength and courage as well as beauty. Apollo had dark gold hair and deep blue eyes, and extraordinary talents in music, poetry, mathematics, and medicine. He became the god of the sun and the patron of the arts and sciences.

Of all the gods he was probably the most admirable, in his character as well as in his appearance. He could not tell a lie, and so the oracle, which he established at Delphi, was sought out by Greek kings and commoners alike to find out what the future held for them. When the oracle agreed to speak, it always told the truth, although often the prophecies foretold danger and disaster and generally the actual prophecy was couched in phrases that were hard to interpret and were often misunderstood by those who heard them.

Apollo preached moderation. He told his followers to look into their own hearts to find the beginnings of wisdom. However, like all of the other gods, he sometimes did not practice what he preached. Occasionally he even angered Zeus with his impetuous behavior. When he became jealous or angry, he, too, could be cruel.

As soon as he was old enough to shoot a golden bow and arrow Zeus had given him, Apollo went in search of Python, the serpent who had tortured his mother. He found the serpent at the foot of Mount Parnassus and raced up the mountain to shoot a burning arrow at the animal, which screamed with pain and fled, leaving a trail of blood behind. The serpent's hiding place was the cave of Mother Earth at Delphi, considered a sanctuary (a place where all fighting had to stop) by gods and man alike. Apollo knew that he could not follow the huge snake into the cave, but he breathed on his arrows and created a smoke screen, which he shot into the entrance of the cave. The cave filled with smoke, and the serpent, suffocating from the fumes, had to crawl out. Apollo shot him full of arrows, skinned him, and kept the hide as a souvenir of his revenge.

But he had accomplished his revenge in a sacred place, and Mother Earth complained to Zeus that her sanctuary had been defiled. To make amends, Apollo instituted annual athletic games at Delphi (which really were meant to celebrate his victory), and named them after his enemy: the Pythian Games. He also established the Delphic oracle and named the priestesses who gave advice Pythonesses. This did not help the dead Python, but the gesture appeased Zeus and got Apollo back into his father's good graces.

Like Zeus, Apollo fell in love with and pursued many women. He also had many children. The most famous was his son Aesculapius, who was gifted with miraculous medical knowledge. Even today, when physicians take the oath to do their best to heal and not harm their patients, they use the name of Aesculapius as a symbol of medical knowledge and skill.

Aesculapius was the son of Apollo and Coronis, a princess of Thessaly. She was in love with a young mortal, but Apollo carried her off with him. While she was pregnant with Apollo's son, she went back to her old lover. Apollo could not bring himself to kill the mother of his unborn child himself, so he asked his sister, Artemis, to shoot her with one of her arrows.

He wanted to save the child, however, so he delivered the baby (probably one of the first surgical births in history) and turned him over to the god Hermes, who was immediately struck by the infant's extraordinary intelligence.

The child was sent to Chiron, a centaur—half man and half horse—until that time the most gifted physician in Greek mythology. Aesculapius soon improved on his master's methods. He doctored everyone who came to him and was able to heal even those who were on the point of death.

Eventually the young doctor enraged Hades, who went to Zeus to complain that Apollo's son was robbing him of his victims at the very point when they were supposed to cross over from the land of the living to the land of the dead. Zeus picked up his thunderbolt and threw it at Aesculapius and the patient he was curing at the time, sending both to Hades.

Apollo was not only heartbroken, but also very angry. He found the Cyclops who had made his father's thunderbolt and killed him, a sin against Zeus that the ruler of the gods could not allow to go unpunished. So he banished Apollo to Hades forever.

Until this time Leto had kept away from Zeus, realizing that Hera was watching her, and that any attempt to get in touch with her children's father could only bring more misfortune on herself. But the banishment of her beautiful and clever son gave her the courage to go to Zeus and remind him of their old love. Zeus listened to her and relented. Not only did he allow Apollo to come back to Mount Olympus, he even agreed to bring Aesculapius back to life, with a warning not to rob Hades by curing those sick humans who were already on their way across the river Styx.

According to one legend, Zeus's reversal of judgment angered Aphrodite. So she ordered Eros to shoot Apollo with the arrow of love, and the mountain nymph, Daphne, who happened to cross his path, with the arrow of indifference. When the beautiful god, not used to being turned down by women, started to follow her, she ran away as fast as she could.

Daphne was the daughter of a river god, and when she realized that Apollo was faster than she, she ran to the river and begged her father to save her. He turned her into a laurel tree. Apollo caught up with the nymph, and found that instead of a beautiful girl, he was hugging a tree with thorns that scratched his face.

So the river god, who knew that Apollo was more powerful than he was and could harm him, gave Apollo a gift to appease him: a crown of laurel leaves. From that day on, crowns of laurel, a plant that would never wither, were awarded to heroes and poets as a sign of extraordinary ability.

Apollo's special friends were the nine Muses, who represented the arts. When he was a very young god, they taught him their skills, so that Apollo became the greatest poet and artist in the universe, improving on everything that the Muses had taught him.

Apollo was one of the few gods who was allowed to keep his original name by the Romans. However, they tended to make him less important than the Greeks had. He was generally pictured as a beautiful young man who somehow never really grew up. Roman statues tend to make him look somehow less masculine than those of the Greeks. His artistic abilities were less respected by the Romans. Music, poetry, and dance were considered among the greatest gifts of the gods by the Greeks, but were generally regarded as entertainment for the masses by the Romans. They respected political and fighting ability in men more than artistic accomplishments.

ARTEMIS

Artemis, Apollo's twin, was, in her own way as beautiful as her brother. While he seemed to be surrounded with a golden light, his sister gleamed like silver. Zeus loved her very much.

On her third birthday, he asked her to make any wish—he would make sure she got what she wanted. Artemis, who, in spite of her youth, had seen all the harm that Aphrodite could do to those over whom she had power, wished that she would always be a young girl—never a woman. She asked Zeus never to give her to any man. Also, she wished for a silver bow and arrow, the best pack of hounds in the universe, and the freedom to run and hunt over the mountains and in the woods for all eternity.

Zeus granted her wishes. He gave her the gift of eternal chastity, but, considering himself more experienced than his three-year-old daughter, told her that she could change her mind about falling in love at any time, if she got tired of the single life.

Artemis went to Hephaestus and asked him to make her a silver bow, but the god of the forge suggested that silver should be created underwater in a cold light. So Artemis swam to the Cyclops who had made Zeus's thunderbolt, and they fashioned for her the most beautiful silver bow, quiver, and arrows in their power. The quiver had a special magic: As soon as it was empty, it filled up again.

Next she visited Pan, who gave her his ten best dogs. From then on Artemis spent her days and nights hunting deer in the woods and streaking across the sky like a silver bolt. She was worshiped as the goddess of the moon and the stars, chaste but happy and fulfilled. Men who came near her, whether they were gods or humans, were frightened away by her fierce hounds.

In many parts of Greece, young women whose relatives wished to marry them off to men they did not love prayed to Artemis to save them. According to legend, she frequently did, although she sometimes had to turn the girl into a tree, a flower, or a deer. But perhaps the Greeks thought that it was preferable to be turned into an enchanted plant or animal than to have to spend the rest of one's life with a mate one disliked.

The Roman name for Artemis was Diana; she became a favorite subject of sculpture and painting. She is usually seen carrying her bow and accompanied by one or more of her many dogs.

Chapter 8 *Aphrodite*

Aphrodite was the goddess of love and beauty, the most enchanting woman in the universe. Some say that she was the daughter of Zeus and Dione, the goddess of the oak tree, but the most popular story is that Aphrodite was born from the foam of the sea, rising naked on a scallop shell, and stepping first on the island of Cythera.

This island was sandy and rocky, with few flowers and birds. But once the goddess set foot on it, it started to bloom, becoming one of the most beautiful places in Greece. However, it seemed like a small place with few opportunities for the young goddess, so she moved on to the island of Cyprus, where hillsides burst into flowers and colorful birds came to sing their songs.

Zeus saw Aphrodite and, because she was the most beautiful being he had ever seen, brought her to Olympus. Hera took one look at her and decided that this goddess would bring nothing but trouble. "Marry her off immediately," she said to Zeus. "If you don't, there will be endless wars and battles over who should gain possession of Aphrodite." For once Hera was right. Aphrodite was lovely to look at, but faithless, vain, and treacherous as well. The gods, however, saw only her beauty, and almost every god offered his most prized possessions to gain her hand in marriage.

Poseidon said he would make her queen of the sea and give her coral palaces, pearls, and mysterious riches that no one on earth knew about. He even promised her the power of life and death over sailors and fishermen who worked on the sea. But riches and power, except the power to seduce all men who came near her, did not interest Aphrodite, so she said no to Poseidon.

Apollo and Hermes also presented themselves as suitors, but she just smiled at them and said nothing.

Hera, who had been watching Zeus out of the corner of her eyes, saw him getting more and more interested in the lovely newcomer. No time, she felt, should be lost in getting Aphrodite as far from her husband's throne as possible. So she brought Hephaestus, the lame and ugly god of the forge, from his workshop at the other end of Olympus, and suggested that such a hardworking, down-to-earth man would make an excellent husband for a flighty woman like Aphrodite. Zeus finally agreed to the match.

Aphrodite accepted the god of the forge, partly because he promised to make her the most beautiful jewelry ever seen in the universe, including a girdle that would make her even more irresistible than she already was, and partly because she felt that he would not watch her too closely and she could have love affairs with others.

And that is exactly what happened. Aphrodite spent all of her time flirting and making love. Soon after her marriage she had three children. The father was not Hephaestus, but the fierce, aggressive, and quarrelsome god of war, Ares. Her husband at first knew nothing of the deception. It was one of the minor gods, Helios, who told Hephaestus about his wife's unfaithfulness.

He decided to trap her. He wove a net, fine as a spider's but quite unbreakable, and placed it around her chamber. Then he told her he was going on a trip. She invited Ares to come to visit, but Hephaestus, who had been watching his wife, stormed into her room, bringing all the other gods with him. He told Zeus that he did not want his unfaithful wife any longer, that he would give her back to him, but that he also wanted the return of all the valuable gifts he had made for Zeus on the occasion of his marriage. Zeus did not want to return the gifts, but several of the other gods said that they would give him the equivalent of the presents if they could have Aphrodite, unfaithful or not, as a wife.

The gods, including Poseidon, Ares, Dionysus, and Hermes, all competed for her, and she had love affairs with all of them, bearing several of them children.

However, Aphrodite, besides being able to attract all gods and humans with her beauty, had one other quality no divine or mortal being has had before or since. She could bathe in the sea and become a virgin again, no matter how many lovers or children she had had. So eventually, Hephaestus, who had never stopped loving her even though he knew her true nature, took her back as his wife.

Aphrodite never changed. According to some legends, the fates had decreed that she would never accomplish anything but to make men love her. But even love can become boring, if that is the only purpose of one's life. So one day Aphrodite, who had watched Athena weave and spin, decided she would try her hand at making a beautiful cloak. Athena caught her at a loom and complained to Zeus. "Is it not enough that every man in the world loves her? Must she also be allowed to take on a task that is my special assignment?" Athena asked Zeus. Zeus forbade Aphrodite from ever doing the work of any other god or goddess again, and made her apologize to Athena.

So perhaps Aphrodite was not really at fault for her unfaithful and flighty nature. After all, the fates had left her nothing to do but to make love. That may also be the reason why her husband continued to stay faithful to her and to keep her. He, too, may have realized that Aphrodite was paying a heavy price for her unparalleled beauty and her ability to attract the love of any male who saw her.

Among Aphrodite's many children was one who, like his mother, used love to make mischief among humans and gods.

Eros (called Cupid by the Romans) was a small boy who never grew up. His mother gave him a bow with a set of two arrows. One kind of arrow, if shot into the heart, would infect the victim with undying love; the other would produce undying indifference. Eros often amused himself by aiming the love arrow at one person and the indifference arrow at another. Then he would make sure that they met. The love-struck person would spend his or her life in pursuit of the perpetually indifferent one, and Eros would stand by laughing.

The Greeks generally considered Aphrodite a dangerous and spiteful goddess, in spite of her great beauty. This was a reflection of the way they looked at love between men and women: sometimes bringing great happiness, but often leading to sorrow or even tragedy. In Greek eyes, friendship between members of the same sex was considered more lasting and reliable than romantic love between men and women.

It is interesting to note that in no legend does Aphrodite show the slightest respect or friendship for another woman. The goddesses on Olympus all despised her, and human women tended to fear her. In spite of her great beauty, the goddess of love was not really loved by anyone, because underneath her beauty was a mean-spirited, jealous, and vain person who caused endless misery. She was, in the end, the goddess who caused the greatest of Greek tragedies: the Trojan War.

The Romans, who called Aphrodite Venus, saw her as being less cruel and deceitful than the Greeks did, and allowed her to help young lovers almost as often as she made them miserable. This reflected their view of humanity. The Romans were more optimistic about male-female relationships than the Greeks were, and many of the early Greek love stories (which exist only as fragments in Greek literature, and often have unhappy endings) were turned into great poems by the Roman writers Ovid and Virgil, with much happier conclusions.

Several modern psychologists have used Aphrodite as a symbol of erotic love, emphasizing both the beauty and the danger these feelings represent for human beings. Sigmund Freud, the father of psychoanalysis, saw her symbolically as the most important of all life forces. Another psychologist, Carl Jung, saw her as the spirit that makes possible man's lively, fruitful, and passionate relationships.

Chapter 9 *Ares*

Of the three unpleasant children Zeus and Hera produced, Ares was the least attractive. As a matter of fact, Greek legends do not allow him one kind act or place him in one sympathetic situation. He is always a complete villain.

He was the god of war, and although occasionally described as good-looking in a sinister kind of way, he is usually pictured as bloodstained, with a murderous expression on his face. Homer calls him murderous and the incarnate curse of the human race. He even describes him as a coward, who bellows in pain and runs away when wounded.

His steady companion was his equally obnoxious sister, Eris (which means discord), who laughed with joy during the bloodiest battles and who never showed any mercy to either side in a conflict.

One may wonder what Aphrodite, the goddess of love, saw in this particular god, since she chose him as one of her many lovers. The children she had with him apparently all took after their father in appearance and character.

The Greeks disliked Ares, but they did not seem to fear him. There were no altars to him, and there is no city in which he was worshiped as one of the principal gods. His favorite animal was, fittingly enough, the vulture.

The Romans, who called him Mars, changed both his appearance and his character for the better, perhaps because they saw more glory and less horror in war. To them he appeared as a god in shining armor, invincible and strong. And he never ran away or whined when he was wounded. They did not build any special temples to him, but they gave him the dog, rather than the vulture, as his special animal.

Chapter 10 *Dionysus*

SOURCES: There are some questions among experts on ancient Greek mythology as to whether Dionysus even belonged to the royal family of gods. Homer did not consider him a proper god. There is no early mention of his name in written texts. Hesiod, in the seventh or eighth century, briefly talks about him. But even the oldest stories about him seem not to have been written down until much later in Greek literary history. Euripides, the most modern of the Greek dramatists, was the first to tell the story of the pirate ship with the mysterious, beautiful young man, who turned out to be the son of Zeus by an earthly maiden.

THE STORY: Dionysus was said to be the son of Zeus and the princess of Thebes, Semele, who had no divine origins herself. So the child was half human, and considered by the other gods to be at least semimortal.

Semele met the same fate as all the other women with whom Zeus fell in love. Hera hated her, and was determined to destroy her.

Zeus was so fascinated by Semele that he told her he would do anything she asked, and swore by the river Styx (an oath that not even the king of the gods could break) that he would grant her any wish. Hera used this promise to her advantage. She came to Semele in a dream and whispered to her that no mortal had ever seen Zeus in his true divine form. Would it not be an incredible honor to be the first to see the king of heaven as only the gods could see him? Semele listened to Hera's treacherous advice. Again, hubris was a factor. She thought that because Zeus loved her she could come to no harm, even though she was only a mortal woman.

She asked her lover to appear to her as he really was. Zeus tried to dissuade her, because he knew that no mortal could see him in his fiery glory and live, but Semele insisted. Since Zeus had sworn that holy oath, he had to comply, and when he appeared in the terrible aspect of his godly power, she died of the shock.

Zeus knew that Semele was pregnant, and he did not want her unborn child to die with her. So he kept it by him, hiding it from Hera until the time came for it to be born. It was a son, and Zeus turned him over to Hermes to carry to the nymphs of Nysa, a place where the finest grapes in all the universe eventually grew.

There is another, much more cruel version of the story, which shows Hera as an even more vicious goddess than most other legends. According to this legend, she found the baby boy, siezed him, and tore him to shreds. Then she boiled him in a cauldron. Pomegranate and grape vines sprouted from the soil where his blood had fallen.

According to this legend, Rhea, the mother of Zeus, made one of her brief reappearances, and, with her godly powers, reconstituted Dionysus into a little boy. Zeus then had Hermes temporarily transform him into a ram and turned him over to the nymphs to care for, thus escaping Hera's wrath. In many sculptures and paintings Dionysus is shown as a man with horns on his head, probably left over from the time he spent as a young ram.

Dionysus grew into a young man who found that he loved travel and adventure. He wandered all over the earth, and taught humans how to turn the juice of grapes into an intoxicating beverage called wine.

Once he sailed with a band of sailors, who did not recognize him as a god. They assumed from his appearance that he was the son of a king, and that, if they captured him and held him for ransom, they would be paid in vast riches. So they seized Dionysus, but no ropes or leather thongs would hold him. All bonds the kidnappers tried to use fell apart as soon as they touched his body. While they were attempting to tie him down, he just laughed at them. One of the kidnappers realized that they were not dealing with an ordinary mortal; he tried to warn his fellows to let the strange young man go free or some serious disaster might befall them. No one paid any attention to him.

Then, even though the wind filled the sails of the ship, the ship would not move. It stood still as if held by hundreds of heavy anchors. Wine started to rain from the heavens, and grape vines grew from the wooden planks of the ship and wound themselves around the masts and the sails.

The terror-stricken would-be kidnappers tried to release their captive, but by now he had turned himself into a lion and roared at them so fiercely that they all abandoned ship. As they hit the water, they became dolphins. Only the one sailor who had tried to dissuade his fellows from their criminal activity was saved by Dionysus. The god carried him to the nearest shore and allowed him to go home to his family.

As he grew older, Dionysus longed for the mother he had never seen. He decided to go on a pilgrimage to the underworld and bring her back with him. When he found her, he defied the power of Hades and all of his cohorts and carried her away from the land of death. But, because she was mortal, he feared that she might die again, so he took her up to Olympus, where the gods (presumably with a negative vote from Hera) allowed her to stay: the only mortal to live among the immortals forever.

The Greeks recognized early that alcohol was a mixed blessing. It could make them feel happy and help them enjoy their festivals. In the days before painkilling medications, it might be used to help the suffering of the sick. But wine, especially too much of it, could also drive drinkers to irrational deeds, and chronic abusers to insanity.

So Dionysus was always considered a god with a double nature: He could be kindly and helpful, and he could add a great deal of joy to festivals held in his honor. But he could be terribly cruel and destructive. In many legends, he is followed by a group of women, the Maenads, who were often frenzied with drink and sometimes tore innocent victims limb from limb. (See Chapter 26, "Orpheus and Eurydice.") When not overcome by wine, the Maenads could behave like perfectly normal women. They lived in the wilderness, and Dionysus made sure that they had plenty of fruit, herbs, and goat's milk to keep them well fed. It was only when they overindulged in wine that they went on their rampages.

Still other, and probably much later, legends connect Dionysus with death and resurrection. Possibly based on the early story of his death at the hands of Hera and rescue by Zeus, or on the idea that he saved his mother from Hades, he became to some Greeks a symbol of eternal life.

Still another explanation of the resurrection symbolism comes directly from nature: The vines that grew grapes had to be pruned back severely every fall in order to grow luxuriantly in the spring and summer and produce a fall harvest. So the wine god might be cut down every winter to return every spring in all his full beauty.

The Romans, especially in the declining years of their empire, concentrated on the intoxicating aspects of Dionysus's power. They called the god Bacchus, and festivities that featured all kinds of excesses in food and drink as well as sexual orgies were called Bacchanalias. Many activities that would have been considered illegal and punished at other times were condoned during the festivals held in honor of Bacchus.

There were also, it seemed, sects who worshiped Dionysus as a deity promising immortality of a different and better kind than the ghostly existence in Hades. Around the year A.D. 80 a Greek writer, Plutarch, wrote a letter to his wife when their little daughter, whom both had loved dearly, died while he was far away from home. "About what you have heard, dear heart, that the soul once departed from the body vanishes and feels nothing, I know that you give no belief to such assertions because of those sacred and faithful promises given in the mysteries of Bacchus, which we who are in that religious brotherhood know. We hold it firmly for an undoubted truth that our soul is incorruptible and immortal. We are to think of the dead that they pass into a better place and happier condition."

This happer-life-after-death religion was obviously not what most Greeks believed, but since Plutarch refers to a "religious brotherhood," we may suppose that there were others who had similar non-Christian ideas about the immortality of the soul.

Chapter 11 *Hades*

When the lots were drawn to determine who would rule the various parts of the universe, Hades was the least lucky. He got what nobody else wanted: the land of the dead, the underworld. He was already gloomy by nature, however, so in a way he was the right choice for the dark kingdom.

Unlike Poseidon—who proceeded immediately to build beautiful castles in the ocean—Hades did little to improve the environment of Hades. The great palace he built was made of black rock and was surrounded by fields called Erebus. There were no flowers or any other kinds of plants in these fields, and no birds ever lived there. However, the souls who spent eternity in Hades often heard the fluttering of wings, and when they did, they shuddered. Hades' companions in his world were the Erinyes, or Furies. Huge, they had large wings with snaky hair, red eyes, and yellow teeth. Their wings were like metal whips, which they occasionally used to kill humans who had displeased them.

The Greeks were so afraid of them that they never called them by their real names. Instead, they were generally referred to as "the Eumenides," which means "the kindly ones." Obviously, people thought flattering these terrible creatures would somehow keep them at bay. But they still appeared regularly on earth, sometimes to punish a human being who had displeased the gods, and sometimes to urge even a guiltless person into madness and suicide.

There were other frightening creatures in the underworld. There was Charon, who rowed the ferry that transported those who had recently died from the land of the living to the underworld. Charon required payment for his ferry service, and the Greeks often buried their dead with a coin under the tongue to make sure that they had the proper fare. Dead souls who could not pay were kept on the wrong side of the river, in a kind of no-man's-land, and might return to haunt the living.

Once the souls had crossed the river, they found the way guarded by the three-headed dog Cerberus, who would attack any living being trying to get into Hades. Sometimes he even ate an intruder.

None of the gods liked Hades. Since he was the brother of Zeus and Poseidon, they could not forbid him to visit Olympus occasionally, but he was never made really welcome. This embittered him even more, and sometimes he tried to kidnap a god's favorite to take back to the underworld.

His best-known victim was the beautiful Persephone, the daughter of Demeter and Zeus (more about that story in Chapter 19).

The Romans changed the name of Hades to Pluto, but otherwise did little to change his character. They continued to call the underworld realm he ruled Hades, and so eliminated the confusion between the name of the ruler and the land that he ruled.

Chapter 12 *Hermes*

Hermes was another of his sons that Zeus favored. Hermes' mother was Maia, the daughter of Atlas the Titan, who after the defeat of his armies had been condemned to carry the universe on his shoulder.

Zeus gifted Hermes with a special lightness. He had wings on his feet and on his helmet, and could fly easily anywhere in the universe. He was also unusually precocious. Five minutes after his birth he sneaked out of his crib and toddled down Mount Olympus, to a place where he found a herd of beautiful white cows grazing in a meadow. It so happened that the herd belonged to Apollo. Crows nesting in the trees told Hermes whose property he was watching. But this did not bother the infant god one bit. He took them anyway.

When Apollo came looking for his cows, the crows told him that a tiny infant had taken them away. That story seemed ridiculous to Apollo, so he went searching for the cows on Olympus and in the woods and meadows nearby.

Soon he came to a cave where the lovely Maia was sitting with a small baby on her lap. "Let me introduce you to your new half-brother, Hermes," she said. "He is the cleverest baby that ever was. Look, he has made a musical instrument out of a tortoise shell and strung it with cow gut. Does it not make beautiful sounds?"

"Where did that infant get cow gut?" asked Apollo, who was finally beginning to believe what the crows had told him. Hermes stood up on his mother's knee and confessed. "I took a herd of white cows, but although the crows told me that they belonged to you, my brother, I did not believe them. I thought they had lost their way and were nobody's property. So I sacrificed them all to the twelve important gods because I wanted to begin my life with an act of worship."

"What *twelve* gods?" asked the astonished Apollo. "As far as I know there are only *eleven*, myself included." "Well, you have just met the twelfth," Hermes told him. "It's me." Apollo was so amused by his infant brother's conceit that he did not even get angry. And, to make up for what he had done, Hermes made Apollo a special lyre. Then he proceeded to cut some reeds and made himself a flute that made sounds almost as lovely as those of the lyre. Apollo, who was, after all, the god of music, recognized talent when he heard it and took Hermes to show off his brother's astounding skills to their father, Zeus.

Zeus, most of whose children were not as likable, amusing, or talented as Hermes, carefully hid him away from Hera, but decided that he wanted to keep him on Olympus at least part of the time. To make sure that Hera did not become suspicious, he decided to make Hermes his messenger. And the young god, as he grew into manhood, became very useful to his father.

When Hades threatened to tell Hera the truth about Hermes, who was understandably afraid of her, he agreed to serve as a messenger for the underworld as well. Occasionally, when not occupied with pleasant tasks for his father, he would also act as a guide to speed dead and dying mortals to the underworld.

The cleverness he had shown as an infant grew along with his body. He built himself a workshop on Olympus and invented the alphabet, astronomy, and the scales. To amuse himself, he also devised any number of card games and became an expert cheat.

Because of his many talents, he was named the god of gamblers and thieves, but also the protector of commerce and the guardian of travelers.

The Greeks apparently saw that an individual who was expert at dealing with money and other worldly goods might use his talents for both good and evil, for honorable occupations and for crime.

Hermes, because of his beauty and his picturesque attire, was a favorite subject of painters and sculptors, although he, like Ares, had no special temples or cities.

The Romans called him Mercury. Most Roman tales about him emphasize his speed and his skills as a messenger and ignore his double nature. Commerce and industry were too important to the Romans to want a god who was both a merchant and a thief.

Chapter 13 *Hephaestus*

Hephaestus was Hera's first child. She awaited his birth with joy, expecting him to outshine all of the children Zeus had already fathered with other women. But when the baby was born, he was not only ugly, but deformed as well. Hera felt no love for him. She did not even wait for her husband to see his son; she hurled him off Olympus.

According to one legend, he hurled through space for a night and a day, and finally hit the ground at the edge of the ocean. He had been injured severely and cried piteously. Had he been a mortal infant, he would, of course, have been killed by the fall. But because he was a god, he was immortal.

A kindly water nymph, Thetis, found him and took pity on the infant. She kept him in her grotto, where he amused himself playing with shells and bright stones and pebbles. As he grew older, he showed an amazing talent for making these objects into beautiful jewelry.

One day Thetis happened to show Hera a lovely brooch her foundling had made. Hera had heard the story of the infant the nymph had adopted and decided that this must be the son she had disowned. Because he was so very talented, and because Hera wanted to possess his unique jewels, she demanded that his adoptive mother send him back to Olympus. But she still did not want to have her ugly son nearby.

She found him a mountain with a large hole in the center, and set him up there, giving him forges and bellows so that he could perfect his craft. Some of the Cyclops (who, of course, were even uglier than he was) were delegated to be his helpers.

Zeus, who may or may not have known that Hephaestus was actually his son, came to respect him very much when he saw the strong and useful weapons that he could design and produce.

Hephaestus was a kindly and artistically gifted god, who even loved his cruel mother and his faithless wife, Aphrodite. Often, when Zeus got angry at Hera for meddling in his affairs, Hephaestus tried to protect her, but she never showed him the slightest love or gratitude.

The Roman name for Hephaestus was Vulcan. In their country, a mountain that rumbled and sometimes spit out fiery smoke and lava was thought to be the place in which Vulcan worked on his forge.

Sculptures of this god show him as deformed—often with one

leg shorter than the other, and occasionally with a humped back—but his face often looks rather kind, perhaps like that of a local armorer or goldsmith who was not an aristocrat, but a hardworking tradesman of humble origin.

Chapter 14 *Hestia*

Hestia was Zeus's sister. Like Athena and Artemis, she was a virgin goddess. In spite of her single state, she was considered the goddess of home and hearth. One ancient custom, which still persists in some Greek villages, was to carry a newborn child around the home fire before it was received into the family.

From very early times, Greek cities established a community hearth and fire that was sacred to Hestia, with an eternal flame that was never allowed to go out. When a new city or village was founded, the colonists would carry smoldering coal from their old home to the new one to start a fresh fire. This was one of the earliest recorded Greek customs.

Since the guardian of the home was too sacred to be gossiped about, there are few stories about Hestia, and she has no particular personality. Perhaps, too, this is a reflection of the way ancient Greek men viewed family life. Men and women generally lived quite separate existences, and the children were considered mainly the responsibility of the women in the household. When boys grew up, they joined the company of men and generally lived separately from their mothers and sisters.

In Rome, Hestia's name was changed to Vesta, and she was important in both private and public worship. Her fire was cared for by six virgin priestesses, who were chosen from some of the city's most important families. These women often had great influence in politics, and were considered to have the gift of prophecy by some of Rome's later rulers. However, a Vestal virgin who lost her virginity was punished by death, because the Romans believed that her sin would bring disaster on the city.

Chapter 15 *Pan*

Pan was considered a god, even though he was never allowed on Mount Olympus, and even though, according to most legends, he died of a mysterious illness and therefore was definitely not immortal.

Hermes was said to have been his father, but no two legends agree about his mother. At any rate, he was born half-human and half-goat. Apparently he managed to grow into manhood on his own, and lived most of his life in meadows and woodlands the Greeks called Arcadia.

He was a happy, noisy god, who made his home among the herds of animals he resembled. But, being the son of Hermes, he also had one divine talent: He was a superb musician. He fashioned a musical instrument out of graduated reeds, which looked like a tiny pipe organ, but which he used like a flute. On it he could play melodies that beguiled gods and humans alike.

His playmates were the nymphs of the countryside, who loved his music and laughed at his jokes, but who thought him too ugly to love or marry. Pan was always in love with one or more of these nymphs, but the fact that they all turned him down does not seem to have depressed his spirits unduly.

The news that Pan had died was told by the winds to a sailor, Thamus, on a ship bound to Italy. Some legends indicate that the winds were informed by Hermes that his son had died, and that, although he had not paid much attention to him while he was alive, he did not want to let his passing go unnoticed.

At any rate, Thamus told his fellow sailors that while he stood watch in a storm at the helm of his ship, he heard the winds shout, "Thamus, are you there? When you reach port, take care to proclaim that the great god Pan is dead. . . ." Thamus did as he was told, and many lamented Pan's death. Some shepherds or goat breeders, whose patron he had been, refused to believe that story. Long after Pan had supposedly passed from earth to Hades, they still took care of his altars, which were built in wilderness grottos.

In a way, this very earth-bound god was more real to the people who lived in the countryside than many of the great gods of Olympus, who would have been much too proud to share their humble occupations and cares.

One sculptor's idea of
how Apollo looked. The statue
is in the Vatican museum in Rome.

A very ancient statue of Apollo, in the Louvre in Paris.

*The head of the same ancient Apollo statue.
Many of today's art historians think
that this simple, beautiful style of sculpture
has influenced much of modern art.*

Stone lions guard the island of Delos, where it is said Apollo was born.

Sculptures of deer guard the harbor at Rhodes. The deer was an animal sacred to the goddess Artemis, the twin sister of Apollo.

A statue of Athena in a museum in Naples, Italy.

Hera was a very unpopular goddess, both on Mount Olympus and, apparently, among the Greeks. There are very few statues of her anywhere. However, the peacock, her sacred bird, can be found almost everywhere.

Jason and the Golden Fleece. In the Borghese Gardens in Rome.

The weapons that Neptune used to spear fish are still seen on today's fishing boats in a Greek harbor.

Neptune. This statue can be seen in the Louvre in Paris.

The Acropolis in Athens.

Mercury, on his way to deliver a message. The statue is in a museum in Florence, Italy.

Aphrodite holding the fatal golden apple, awarded to her by Paris when he chose her as the most beautiful goddess of all . . . and started the events that led to the Trojan War tragedy.

Paris, a weak and undiplomatic young man, whose thoughtless act—awarding the golden apple to Aphrodite in the beauty contest of the goddesses—caused tragedy to himself, his family, and his country.

Even though there are few heroines in Greek myths, women must have been considered important by some. Female figures, instead of columns, hold up the roof of the Erechtheum, a small temple near the Parthenon.

A detail of the Parthenon in Athens.

A tomb in which Queen Clytemnestra is said to be buried. Clytemnestra may have been a fictitious character, but the tomb looks at once regal and stark . . . a fitting resting place for a tragic and murderous woman.

The view from a hill, where, according to local legend, Agamemnon's castle stood. From this spot Clytemnestra, the wife who hated and feared him, waited with murder in her heart for his return from Troy. Even today, the arid, windswept, deathly quiet valley weaves a mysterious and frightening spell.

PART THREE

Man's Fate

Chapter 16

Prometheus:

The First of the Great Heroes

SOURCES: Fragments from Hesiod; the drama *Prometheus Bound*, by Aeschylus.

THE STORY: Zeus did not create man. By the time the chief of the gods had overthrown his father and established himself as the ruler of Olympus, humans were already well entrenched on earth, a fact that Zeus occasionally regretted.

He worried about mankind. Might humans someday become powerful enough to compete with the gods? Were these human creatures getting above themselves? Were they not respectful enough and in sufficient awe of the gods? Occasionally an individual or group of humans would do, or fail to do, something that enraged Zeus. For instance, one group of humans decided, perhaps because they felt that the gods needed food less than they themselves did, to keep the best part of their animal sacrifices for themselves, and offer to Zeus only those bits and pieces that were tough or not very tasty. According to one set of legends, Zeus decided (with the help of Poseidon) to let loose a flood upon mankind and wipe out everybody except one pious couple who had always offered Zeus the best of the sacrifices, keeping only the entrails of the animals for themselves.

At any rate, humankind grew in numbers, but not in knowledge and power, because Zeus had kept one very important element confined to Olympus and the gods alone: fire. Without fire, man could not cook food, could not make weapons or create new inventions. To the gods, fire represented knowledge and inventiveness. As long as men were kept cold and ignorant, they were no threat to the Olympians.

There was one member of the Olympian community who did not agree with this policy—Prometheus. He was a Titan. When his brothers and cousins fought Zeus to keep Cronus in power, Prometheus, who considered Cronus a heartless tyrant, had sided with Zeus and had even stood by while his friends and relatives were exiled or killed after Cronus's defeat. He had expected Zeus to be a better ruler—fairer and kinder to mankind—than he turned out to be.

Repeatedly Prometheus begged Zeus to give humans fire, to allow them knowledge and light. Zeus always refused, and Prometheus began to see that Zeus had become the same kind of tyrant his father had been.

So one evening, when everyone on Olympus was sleeping, Prometheus took a twig and held it to some Olympian smoldering coals until it caught fire. He took that twig and carried it down to earth. Before turning over the power of this formerly divine element to humans, he carefully explained that it could be used for both good and evil. Fire could bring warmth and light. It could produce objects that might make life on earth much more bearable. But it could also bring death and destruction. Humankind would have to use its new power thoughtfully and carefully. With knowledge came responsibility, he explained. And with responsibility came the loss of a certain kind of innocence that goes with powerlessness. Mankind promised to use fire wisely, though as we know, the promise has not always been kept. The fire that warms our homes and fuels our industry is the same flame that creates our ability to destroy ourselves. Zeus's fury at the disobedient Titan had no bounds, and he devised a terrible punishment for Prometheus. He was chained to a rock jutting out of the ocean in the coldest part of the universe. Prometheus was immortal, so he could not die. However, he could suffer the most hideous kind of pain forever. Zeus ordered vultures to claw at and eat Prometheus's liver every day. Every night, in the freezing cold, the liver would grow back, only to be torn away again the next day.

There was a way in which Prometheus might have saved himself. Zeus thought that the Titan knew who would eventually replace Zeus as the ruler of the universe. Because Zeus had killed his own father, he feared that someday one of his sons might kill him. So if Prometheus would tell what he knew, Zeus would release him from his torment. But Prometheus refused to do what Zeus wanted. He also refused to apologize for giving fire to mankind. So, according to some legends, he was eternally damned to a life of unbelievable pain because he would not give in to a tyrant god's demands. In other legends, he does eventually tell Zeus what he wanted to know and is released. Yet other stories say Hercules rescued him.

Aeschylus, according to historical record, wrote a trilogy about Prometheus. The first of the three plays is called *Prometheus Bound*, and tells of the hero's suffering and defiance. The other two dramas are lost to us. They were called *Prometheus Unbound* and *Prometheus, the Fire Bearer*. From the title of the second play, we can deduce that, according to Aeschylus, Prometheus was rescued from his horrible fate. The last play may have been a glorification of Prometheus as the hero of the universe: a religious play that lauded the Titan who fought the tyranny of Zeus and submitted to infinite suffering to benefit mankind. It may even have suggested that Prometheus himself was the one who replaced Zeus.

There are some historians who suspect that the second and third plays may have vanished because the authorities in Athens did not look kindly on such revolutionary writings. We think of Athens as the first democracy, but it was a democracy without a Bill of Rights. Freedom of speech, press, and religion did not exist. There was strict censorship of what could and could not be published or performed. It is entirely possible that the kings of Athens, who saw the power of Zeus over Olympus as a reflection of their own power over their city, did not like the idea of a play that dealt with the heroic defeat of tyranny.

Through the centuries Prometheus has always had a special appeal for writers and artists who loved freedom and hated tyranny. One of the last works of the English poet Percy Bysshe Shelley was his own version of *Prometheus Unbound*. In his notes he explained that he considered Prometheus one of the greatest of freedom-loving heroes in literature, and Zeus (or Jupiter, as he referred to him) as a tyrannical oppressor. He felt that he wanted to continue the Prometheus story as, he said, Aeschylus had done in the lost plays. So, Shelley, in his play, had Prometheus freed by a group of spirits who proved to be more powerful than Jupiter himself, while mankind and all of nature rejoiced. This was a much more optimistic and romantic view of fate and the world than the Greeks had. They were basically cynical and had considerably less faith in the triumph of good over evil than did the nineteenth-century English romantic poets.

There are other ways in which Prometheus the freedom fighter is celebrated. When the skaters at New York City's Rockefeller Center look up at that shining golden figure above their heads, they may not know who that beautiful young man is, especially when he is surrounded by holiday lights, as he is during each Christmas season. But even those visitors to New York who have never heard of Prometheus and his struggle with Zeus see him as a figure of light, shining out of the darkness. Perhaps that is the way the Titan who gave man fire, and thus the knowledge and power to build such works as Rockefeller Center, would like to be remembered.

Chapter 17

Pandora: The First Woman?

Condemning Prometheus for giving fire (and thus knowledge and power) to mankind did not satisfy Zeus. Although apparently nobody had bothered to let humans know that they should not accept the gift, Zeus decided to punish them as well.

He ordered Hephaestus to make a young woman out of clay, using his wife, Aphrodite, as the model. Then he breathed life into the clay figure, along with foolishness and vanity as her principal attributes, besides her extraordinary beauty. He even ordered the other gods to help him make her the most desirable woman in the universe. Athena was asked to teach her to spin and weave, although not to give her any wisdom. Demeter taught her how to grow lovely flowers. Presumably, Aphrodite taught her how to use her female attractions to the best advantage when dealing with men. Hera, on the other hand, was asked to give her a few undesirable qualities: an insatiable curiosity and a suspicious mind.

Then Hermes, at the request of Zeus, presented the woman, who was named Pandora, with a gorgeous golden box. She was instructed never to open it under any circumstances. Hermes warned her that terrible events would occur if she ever lifted the lid of that magic box.

There are two versions of how Pandora got to earth from Olympus to bring disaster to humankind. The first is that, until her arrival, there had been *no* women. Though how the human race reproduced itself and multiplied, where all those men came from, is never explained. Men had lived happily and harmoniously (though, presumably, before the arrival of fire, ignorant and powerless) in an earthly paradise. There was no illness, no suspicion, no jealousy, no discord. Then suddenly this gorgeous creature was deposited among all the happy men by Hermes, at Zeus's orders. All men immediately wished to possess her, and the seeds of discord were already sown.

In a second version of the myth, Pandora was taken to Epimetheus, the brother of Prometheus, with a message from Zeus that he had selected this most beautiful creature to be Epimetheus's wife, as a sort of apology for being overly strict with his brother. This legend, of course, does not mention that Pandora was the first woman. If the concept of marriage existed, then there had to be other women already on earth.

At any rate, both legends agree on one point: Pandora spent much of her time on earth looking at the forbidden box, attempting to figure out why she had been ordered not to open it. The suspiciousness that had been put into her mind by Zeus and Hera made her wonder if it contained some valuable property, perhaps some special magic, that the father of the gods wanted to keep from her. Her foolishness allowed her to think that nothing terrible could happen to her because she was so beautiful. And her insatiable curiosity did not allow her to sleep night or day, wondering what was hidden in that box.

One day she decided that she could not stand the suspense any longer. She took the small golden key that had been given her by Hermes, fitted it into the keyhole, and turned it. Then she gently opened the lid.

First she heard a rustling and smelled a disgusting odor. And then, before she could slam the lid shut again, a host of hideously ugly lizards, snakes, and insectlike creatures swarmed out, hissing and making other horrid sounds. They flew around her head, and then off in all directions. Pandora realized at once that she had made a terrible mistake, and she shut the box as quickly as she could, but only one creature was trapped inside.

What were these hideous, terrible creatures Pandora had loosed upon the world? They were all the ills that beset mankind. The creatures were illness and strife and envy and old age and pain and sorrow and famine. Those were the qualities Zeus decided humanity deserved because they had accepted knowledge that, according to him, was not suitable for mortals.

But it all could have been worse. The creature that Pandora had managed to trap inside was foreboding, the ability to know ahead of time exactly what misfortune would happen to one from the day one was born to the day one died. With foreboding, hope would have been impossible, and without hope we cannot live.

According to some legends, the one creature who did not escape was hope itself. And because hope still remains under the control of human beings, they can continue to exist, always believing that tomorrow will be better.

No legend tells us what happened to Pandora after she disobeyed Zeus's command, but presumably she stayed around with the rest of her fellow humans to share in their misfortunes and sorrows. Since she was created as a mortal, she also presumably eventually died and floated forever among the unhappy souls in Hades.

Chapter 18
Poseidon and Demeter

Poseidon was so delighted with his kingdom, the sea, that he built a whole underwater city, including a palace of pearl and coral for himself. He needed a queen, and he chose the most beautiful water nymph, Nereid, as his bride. But he heard a prophecy (some say it came from Hera) that any son Nereid would bear him would be stronger than his father and might even depose him from his watery kingdom.

So, as a second choice, Poseidon picked another water nymph, Amphitrite, who at first was pleased to be crowned queen of the oceans. But she soon came to regret her marriage. Like his brother Zeus, Poseidon was an unfaithful husband. He was constantly running or swimming after beautiful women. He did not spend much time in his kingdom, but traveled constantly through the universe, where he found many beautiful and willing maidens, attracted by his power and riches. According to legend, he had more than one hundred children.

He was also a difficult god, changeable and quarrelsome, who hardly ever forgave a slight. When he got angry, he let loose the waves of the sea to create storms and hurricanes, which could destroy whole parts of the earth. However, none of these powers could reach Olympus, which towered above the waters.

He was a practical joker who liked to frighten other gods and humans by creating monsters like the octopus, the squid, and the blowfish. When he was still in love with his wife, Amphitrite, he made her a beautiful dolphin and gave it to her as a gift. The dolphin was regarded by the ancient Greeks as Poseidon's special pet, and, according to some legends, killing a dolphin was a serious insult to the sea god, bound to bring terrible vengeance.

Soon, however, Poseidon became dissatisfied with owning only the city under the sea and started looking for some earthly properties. He picked a city called Attica, near enough the ocean so that it would be easy for him to reach. He claimed it by planting his trident in a hillside where a salt spring spouted.

But the people of Attica were unhappy with Poseidon as their ruler. They knew him to be cruel and greedy, and they thought that when he was in a bad mood he might well wipe them out with wind and water. So they appealed to Zeus to give them another ruler. Zeus was not listening, but Athena heard their prayer and came down to plant an olive tree right next to the saltwater spring. Poseidon was enraged. He immediately raised a huge storm, which blew a whole fishing fleet out to sea, never to be heard from again.

His vengeful action only made the inhabitants of Attica more certain than before that they did not want him as their special god. They appealed to Zeus again, and he came down to make peace.

First he declared a truce between Poseidon and Athena, and then he called a council of the gods to decide who would be put in charge of Attica. The other gods knew that Athena was more even-tempered and sensible than Poseidon, as well as much wiser. So they voted for her. In gratitude, the citizens changed the name of their town from Attica to Athens, and declared the olive tree sacred to Athena.

But Poseidon did not forgive them. From then on, Athenians had to exercise special care when they went to sea, and many stopped being fishermen and learned other skills and trades. Also, Athens tended to be at a disadvantage in sea battles. Poseidon, remembering how he had been rejected, usually sided with the enemies of Athens.

After Poseidon lost Athens to Athena, he decided that he had better spend more time on Olympus, to make sure that he did not lose any more territory to other gods. While there, his wandering eye fell on Demeter, who was actually his sister. But that made no difference to him. He pursued her anyway.

Demeter wanted nothing to do with her brother god. She knew of his changeable nature, and besides, since she was the goddess of corn and the moon, she had no desire to live underwater. But one evening Poseidon cornered her in a mountain pass and blocked it with his huge body, so that she could not flee. Finally Demeter said, "If you give me a gift, the most beautiful thing on the face of the earth, I will be yours." She had seen some of Poseidon's monster creations and expected that he could not make anything beautiful, no matter how hard he tried.

But Poseidon fooled her. He made a horse, so beautiful that the goddess gasped with wonder. She was still safe from her brother god, however; he had a very short attention span and had become so fascinated by his new creation that he made a whole herd of horses, which galloped around the meadows, tossing their manes and their tails. He was so pleased with his creation that he forgot all about Demeter and leaped on one of the horses to ride away on the wind.

Later he made a herd of small green horses, known as sea horses, which he kept in his underwater kingdom.

According to an earlier legend, Poseidon had previously tried to make a horse but somehow his work of art had not turned out just right. He got the neck too long, creating a giraffe. Or he put humps on the animal's back and got a camel. Once he came close, but the pelt turned out striped, so he had a zebra. He did not kill these creatures, but just let them run away on earth. That is why their offspring are still with us today.

The Romans called Poseidon Neptune. Since much of their fortune, both in commerce and war, depended on the oceans, he was one of their most important gods. In most Roman myths, Neptune is less mischievous and irresponsible than the Greeks' Poseidon. An angry Neptune was to be feared, his wrath to be taken seriously. The storms he created could destroy the Roman navy and lead to losses in peace and war. In Roman sculptures, Neptune tends to loom larger, fiercer, and more majestic than does Poseidon in Greek art. Keeping on Neptune's good side seemed to the Romans a wise political move. Somehow, they did not count on Jupiter or Athena (Minerva in Roman legends) to save them from the sea god's wrath.

Chapter 19

Persephone in Hades

SOURCES: The story of Persephone, daughter of Demeter, who lives on earth during the spring, summer, and early fall, and has to return to Hades for late fall and winter, is one of the earliest of all Greek myths. Similar stories are told in other cultures, by people who lived where there are distinct seasonal changes. The disappearance of a lovely young god or goddess seems to be one of the ways in which ancient cultures explained how the fruitful and sunny spring and summer seasons turn into the bleak winter months. The Greeks, however, were especially ingenious in developing a myth that allows the spring goddess to return annually. Most other cultures just tell how their symbol of spring and summer disappears or is killed, without finding an answer to the problem of having him or her return each year. So their seasonal explanations don't work as well as the one the Greeks devised.

Demeter, Persephone, and Hades have fascinated artists, writers, composers, and choreographers through the centuries. There are many works of art that tell of the young and innocent girl snatched away by the dark god of death. In some versions, although she initially resists being taken from her loving mother and her many friends, she returns to Hades voluntarily for part of every year to comfort the dead shades whom she comes to pity as she gets to know them. The modern French author, André Gide, for instance, used that version in his well-known poem, which was set to music by Igor Stravinsky, and became one of the last ballets choreographed by George Balanchine.

THE STORY: The earth goddess Demeter had only one daughter, a girl of exceptional loveliness whose happy nature delighted everyone who knew her. Her mother doted on her, and, because she knew that many males, both god and human, might be attracted to her and try to take her away, she took exceptionally good care of her.

But a young girl can't always be kept at home, so on an especially warm and enticing morning, Persephone went to pick flowers with some of her friends. She strayed too far into a meadow of narcissus, and was seen by the god of the underworld, Hades, who immediately fell in love with her.

As her friends left her to go back to their homes, he snatched her up and forced her into his bleak carriage, pulled by two huge black horses. He took the crying and protesting young girl to his home in the underworld, where he intended to keep her forever, as queen of his kingdom. But Persephone could not settle down in her new life. She longed for the light, warmth, and happiness she had known. Most of all she longed for her mother, Demeter.

When Persephone did not return home with her friends, Demeter went to search for her. No one seemed to have seen her anywhere. Demeter flew all around the earth, asking everyone who might know, humans and gods, what could possibly have happened to her lost daughter. But, for a whole year, she could not find even one clue. Because she was so desperate and lonely, she forgot to bless the earth and its vegetation. The land, which had been fruitful and blooming, turned into a frozen desert. It was as if there never had been any warmth or light. Humans and gods were upset. But Demeter hardly noticed their pleas to return the earth to its former green and flowering state. She sat wrapped in a dark robe, mourning her daughter. With no crops and no warmth, it looked as if everyone on earth would starve or freeze to death. Zeus looked down and finally decided that he would have to rescue the earth and its inhabitants.

First he sent some of the other gods to Demeter to try to persuade her to take up her role again. But Demeter refused to allow the earth to bear fruit until she had Persephone safely back at home. Finally, Zeus found out where Persephone was and went to see his brother Hades. Hades was ordered to return Persephone to earth immediately. But Hades loved the beautiful, sunny girl and he did not want to give her up. Disobeying Zeus was impossible, however, so he thought of another plan. He gave Persephone a magic fruit, the pomegranate, to eat. He knew that if she ate any of the red seeds she would be forced to return to him for at least part of each year.

Then he allowed Hermes to take Persephone to her mother, who was overjoyed to have her daughter back. Demeter immediately saw to it that the seeds in the ground began to sprout, that the flowers and the trees burst into bloom, and that the sun returned to warm the earth and its people.

But every year in the fall Persephone had to go back to Hades, promising her mother she would be back in four months. The magic of the pomegranate seeds had done its work. And when Persephone left, the earth became cold, the flowers died, and the fruit and grain no longer grew because Demeter again sank back into grief over her absent daughter.

Persephone had learned a great deal from her sojourn among the dead. Although she loved to return to earth, she never forgot the sad shades she left behind her every spring. Compassionate and gentle, she tried to help all those who needed her on earth and in the underworld. Eventually she became one of the most beloved of all beings because, even though she was a goddess and therefore immortal, she also knew death. Ancient Greeks in their final hours often turned for guidance or compassion to the one being who knew both mortality and immortality.

There is, incidentally, a half-humorous addition to the Persephone legend that is told in today's Athens. The fields and woods in which the girl played before she was kidnapped have long since turned into one of Greece's most polluted industrial areas. A cloud of gray smoke hangs over that section, which lies between Athens and the sea. Some Greeks say that the god Hades is getting back at them for persuading Zeus to make him return Persephone by refusing to allow the accumulated smoke and soot to blow away in a clean wind. Or they curse some of those who have built the oil rigs and refineries that cause the pollution as creatures of the revengeful god of the underworld.

PART FOUR

Great Heroes and Heroines

Chapter 20

Perseus and the Medusa: Everybody's Fairy Tale

SOURCES: Only fragments of this tale remain in the original Greek, but the whole tale was written down by Ovid, the Roman writer, who must either have heard several pieces of the story and put them all together, or else read the whole in some poem or document that has been lost to us.

The story of Perseus is the ultimate fairy tale. It has elements from folktales that have been told for centuries, in places that seem to have very little else in common: Germany, Ireland, England, Italy, Greece, and even China and Japan. The story even has a thoroughly un-Greek happy ending: The hero marries the maiden he rescues and, presumably, everybody lives happily ever after. But perhaps that is not the way the original Greek story went. It may have been written that way by Ovid, who (unlike some of his gloomy Greek predecessors) loved happy endings.

THE STORY: King Acrisius of Argos was a weak, vain, and jealous man, and an unpopular ruler. He had one asset: a daughter, Danae, who besides great beauty also had a gentle, kind disposition and great intelligence. Naturally, when she came to marriageable age, suitors flocked to the palace to ask for her hand.

But instead of being glad, Acrisius was worried. What if his son-in-law turned out to be more clever and more popular than he was and took his throne away? He decided to ask the Oracle at

Delphi what the future held for him. The answer he got was even worse than the fate he had feared. "Your daughter will bear a son, and one day that son will kill you," he was told.

Consequently, the king thought that his best insurance would be to lock his daughter up in a brass tower, built with no doors and only one small slit to serve as a source of light and air. The slit was too narrow for anyone, even a small child, to put an arm through. The king surrounded the tower with a high wall topped by sharp spikes, and had it patrolled day and night to make sure that nobody got in or out.

It had occurred to him to have Danae killed outright, but he was afraid that whatever god or goddess had favored her with such exceptional beauty and intelligence might take revenge on him. So this was next best, he decided. Closed in, with no freedom or exercise, very little fresh air, and limited food and drink (crusts of bread and dishes of murky water were passed to her through the slit by the guards), she would die without anyone having to use a sword or a knife or giving her poison.

But somehow Danae did not die. She didn't even get sick. She just became more beautiful every day. The king was suspicious. He watched the brass tower closely through his bedroom window. Occasionally he went and peeked through the slit to make sure that everything was still as he had ordered it: Danae locked up in the small space he had provided for her, with no visitors allowed.

One day on such a visit, to his utter horror, he heard the cry of a small baby. Immediately he had the guards break into the tower and confront Danae. How had she managed to get pregnant or to smuggle the infant into the tower past the guards and his own watchful eyes?

Danae told him a remarkable story. One day, when she had sat crying because she felt so lonely and desperate, a golden shower had rained through the slit in the wall. The golden shower turned into a magnificent young man, obviously a god. He spent several nights with her, and nine months later she bore the baby, a healthy, beautiful little boy.

Now the king felt he was in *real* trouble. If his daughter had become the bride of a god, he certainly could not afford to have her killed. And, if the baby was the son of a divine being, killing him was also out of the question. So he decided to repeat his previous pattern. He would put mother and child in a situation in which they would almost certainly die. If the gods were inclined to blame him, he could always tell them that he had done nothing *directly* to cause the deaths. Why he thought the gods would consider this an acceptable excuse is difficult to understand. Nevertheless, the king ordered Danae and her little son to be taken out of their prison and put in a boat without sails, without oars, without a rudder, and with no food and water. The princess and her baby were set adrift on a stormy night. "If she is indeed under the protection of some god, he may still rescue her," the king said to himself. "But that seems unlikely. I can probably now sleep peacefully again, knowing that there won't be any grandson to kill me."

But the gods did indeed make sure that nothing happened to the princess and her son. The shower of gold had been Zeus himself, and all of the inhabitants of Olympus (except, possibly, Hera) were interested in making sure that the woman and the child, who was, after all, at least a half-god, landed safely. Hermes drove clouds over the little boat to send a gentle rain, giving Danae water to drink. Poseidon provided her with fish to eat. Gentle winds pushed the vessel into a safe harbor where fishing boats were just being prepared for their morning run. A fisherman called Dictys saw the beautiful girl and her child and took them home to his cottage. He and his wife had not been blessed with children, so they looked after Danae and her baby just as parents and grandparents should.

The young woman thrived in an environment of love and affection like none she had ever known. And the little boy, whom she named Perseus, grew into a strong, fearless, yet kind and gentle young man. He had inherited a godlike beauty and intelligence from his father, and all who knew him loved him.

One day, when Danae and her son were accompanying Dictys to the market to help him sell his fish, they were seen by the king of the island (which was called Sephiros). King Polydectes was much like Danae's father: vain, jealous, and cruel. He also had an eye for beautiful women, and he ordered Danae and her son to be removed from the fisherman's cottage, where they had been so happy, and brought to his palace. He wooed Danae, who made it clear that she was not interested in him. When he promised to marry her, she said that she would have to turn him down because all her time, energy, and love were taken up with her son, Perseus. Now getting rid of Perseus became one of Polydectes' main preoccupations.

Although the king made sure that Perseus had no property of his own, the young man was still happy and proud. He loved to listen to the stories his mother told him of monsters and giants and horrible beings whom he hoped someday to be able to defeat with his strength and skill. Among the stories was one of a beautiful young woman called Medusa, who had insulted Athena. Athena turned her into the world's ugliest monster, with bulging eyes, a swollen black tongue that hung from her mouth, yellow fangs instead of teeth, and live, hissing snakes for hair. Indeed, Medusa was so horrible to look at that anyone who saw her face immediately turned to stone. She had two sisters who took Medusa to a secret place near the ends of the earth, where they lived together and plotted ways to avenge themselves on Athena—an impossibility, since Athena was a goddess.

Perseus learned from his mother that there were whole armies of stone figures around Medusa's hiding place—would-be heroes who had tried to rid the world of her, and who had been turned into rocks themselves. Perseus saw the elimination of Medusa as a proper test for himself. One day, he told himself, he would find her and kill her.

On the day of a huge festival, King Polydectes asked those subjects who wished to enjoy his favor to give him valuable presents to celebrate the occasion. It was the custom in that country on such an occasion to offer the best one had to show what a good citizen one was, and to let others see one's power and generosity. Other young men offered Polydectes all kinds of riches, but Perseus had nothing of value to give. Polydectes, who had decided that this was the occasion to humiliate the son of the woman who had spurned him, specifically asked him what kind of present he had brought.

Proud young Perseus could not make himself say that he had absolutely nothing. Instead, he offered what until then had been only a dream: He would bring the head of the Medusa.

Everybody in the crowd laughed. It was well known that the Medusa was very difficult to find and that those who were unlucky enough to reach her never came back. They just became part of her rock garden. Polydectes was delighted. Here was an unforeseen opportunity to get rid of Danae's son.

"Go and get me the head of the Medusa," he said. "If you do, that will be the most magnificent present I have ever received, and you will be considered the bravest, cleverest, and most powerful man in the country."

Perseus knew that he would never be able to fulfill his promise on his own. But he also knew that he was the son of a god, so he climbed up a cliff and implored whatever god was available at the moment to help him. Hermes was sent down by Zeus to help his half-brother, but also to let him know that the kind of promise he had made was unwise. After giving him a brotherly scolding, Hermes informed Perseus that the gods had indeed decided to help him. Zeus was furious at Polydectes for wanting to marry Danae. Athena also took an interest in Perseus's quest. She knew that the Medusa and her sisters hated her, and she hated them in return. So, helping her half-brother kill the Medusa seemed a worthwhile project.

She had originally made the winged sandals that helped Hermes fly over the earth and the oceans with complete ease. Now she made similar ones for Perseus. She also knew an indirect way to get to the Medusa. So she told Hermes to give Perseus the magical sandals, and to point him in the right direction.

"First you have to find three witches we call the Gray Sisters and force them to tell you the whereabouts of the Medusa," he told Perseus. "Of course, we could tell you where the Medusa is right now, but then you would not have to prove your bravery, intelligence, and strength, and Zeus wishes you to do this. So, first fly straight north and find the Gray Sisters. You'll recognize them because they have only one eye and one tooth between them, which they pass around as needed."

Perseus, delighted with his power to fly, made a few passes around the rock on which he was standing, and then came back to thank Hermes properly. He also asked him to give his profound thanks to Athena and Zeus, and promised never, under any circumstances, to allow himself to believe that he could perform miracles without the help of the gods.

After flying due north for several weeks, and managing to cross over high mountains he could never have topped without his magic sandals, Perseus found a deep, craggy valley. There, under a few scraggly bushes, huddled three very old women. They were dressed in gray rags, with gray hair, and gray faces. And they were obviously quarreling. It turned out that each wanted possession of the eye and the tooth, and they were continually snatching these body parts from each other while at the same time screaming curses. Perseus swooped down and got possession of the disputed objects. Without the eye and the tooth, the three old witches were, of course, helpless, and they begged the young man to return them.

He told them that since he himself had two eyes and a full set of teeth, he had no need of their prized possessions, but he would return them only if the women would tell him how to find the Medusa.

"She and her sisters recently moved to the other end of the earth," one of the witches said. "We don't know exactly where you can find them, but we know who can tell you: the Nymphs of the West. They have recently been assigned by Hera to guard a special tree she is trying to hide from Zeus. The tree bears golden apples, which, it is said, can make any mortal woman as beautiful as a goddess. Hera has had enough trouble with mortal women, and she doesn't want Zeus to find the tree, so he can give the apples as presents to anyone he wants. We will let you know where the Nymphs of the West are, and you can try to get them to tell you the Medusa's hiding place. But first, let us warn you—the Nymphs are so beautiful that every man who sees them falls in love with them and never wants to leave. The Nymphs will tease him, and then, as often as not, throw him into the ocean to drown."

"I'm not going to let that worry me," said Perseus. "The gods will protect me from falling in love with the Nymphs who will divert me from finding and killing the Medusa." Then he carefully memorized the directions (to fly west as far as his winged shoes would take him) and gave the tooth and the eye back to the witches as he had promised.

He found the Nymphs. They were guarding the tree with the golden apples on the uttermost western island, so far from Olympus that Zeus had, as yet, not discovered it.

The Nymphs at first mistook Perseus for Hermes, since he was the only young male they knew who owned winged sandals. But even when they found out that their visitor was not the god they thought, they were still enchanted with him. In fact, the usual situation was almost reversed: The Nymphs fell in love with Perseus, while Perseus, intent on his mission, was only interested in finding out where the Medusa was hidden.

The Nymphs tried to persuade him to stay, assuring him that they had no intention of throwing him in the ocean. They even promised that they would let him taste some of Hera's golden apples; but he staunchly turned them down.

"If you really care about me, you'll help me find the Medusa," he told them. "Zeus is tired of having men turned into rocks; and besides, I have sworn a holy oath that I will bring her head to the king of my country."

So, sadly, the Nymphs decided that they would have to let him go. They even gave him two important presents, objects that would help him kill the Medusa without becoming a part of her rock garden. First they gave him a cap that made him invisible. Then they gave him a brightly polished shield, which gleamed like a mirror. They told him to look at the reflection of the Medusa's head in the shield when he attacked her, so he would not be looking directly into her terrible face.

The Medusa, they said, lived on the northern rim of the earth where the sun rarely appeared, and where the winds constantly tore at the few trees and bushes that had managed to survive. There, in a craggy mountain cave, he would find the Medusa and her two sisters.

He flew for many days, but when he came to the valley where

the Medusa and her two sisters were hiding, he knew at once that he had arrived. Thousands of stone figures surrounded the cave where the three sisters lived. Putting on his cap of invisibility, he swooped down on the fierce monster, with his back turned and the shiny side of his shield pointed in her direction. He recognized the Medusa by her snaky hair, but she could not harm him, since he was not looking at her directly. With his sharp, long sword, he chopped off her head, picked it up, and flew away. Her two sisters tried to follow him, but he was too fast for them.

Now his intention was to get back to his island home as quickly as possible, to turn over his prize to Polydectes. On the way, however, he had another adventure. As he flew east, along the shore of the ocean, he saw a beautiful young girl dressed in the finest clothes and decked out in valuable jewels. She was crying bitterly; and no wonder: She was chained to a rock, about two hundred yards from shore. On that shore a crowd of sad-looking people stood watching her.

Perseus decided to interrupt his journey long enough to find out what was wrong. He landed and approached the king and queen (whom he recognized, since they were the only ones wearing crowns). "Why is everybody so sad, and what is that lovely young woman doing out there on the rock?" he asked.

"It's all my wife's fault," said the man with the crown, who was indeed the king of the country, which was called Joppa. "She was exceedingly proud of our daughter Andromeda's beauty. So one day she said that Andromeda was more beautiful than any of the Nereids, who, as you know, are the god Poseidon's favorite mermaids. Not only did she make this boast, but she was stupid enough to do it right near the ocean. One of the mermaids complained to Poseidon, who was furious at my wife's pride. So he created an enormous sea monster, longer than any of our warships, and broader than my palace. He threatened to let this monster come ashore and destroy our country, eating up all the people in it, unless we sacrificed our daughter. We were told to bind her to that rock out there, where the monster will come and eat her."

"Boasting about your daughter by comparing her to immortal

beings was indeed stupid," said Perseus. "But since none of this seems to be your poor daughter's fault, I will kill the sea monster and rescue her. I think that the gods will forgive me; I have a rather special relationship with some of them."

So he flew out over the ocean and stationed himself near the rock. When the huge sea serpent appeared, he put on his cap of invisibility, flew right over the monster's head, and hit it with his sword. The monster screamed, reared up once, and disappeared back into the sea, the water around him turning red with his blood. Perseus untied the girl, who now wept with relief and gratitude, and flew her back to her parents.

He was so struck with her beauty and gentleness that he asked the king for her hand in marriage. Andromeda had never seen so handsome and, she thought, so heroic a man and would have been delighted to become his bride. But the king and queen had apparently learned very little about excessive pride. "*You* marry our only daughter?" the king shouted. "She is beautiful and rich, and could marry any prince in the land. You may be good-looking, and good at swordplay, but you are a nobody from nowhere. We want our child to marry an aristocrat, preferably a king."

"You are about to become my father-in-law, whether you want to or not," Perseus said. "You were perfectly willing to sacrifice your daughter to that awful sea monster to save yourselves, but you won't allow her to marry a man she loves, the man who saved her life. Eventually the gods will probably get you, but meanwhile, good-bye." He picked up Andromeda and flew off toward his homeland.

When he landed on the island where he had left his mother and Polydectes, he was amazed to find most of it deserted. With Andromeda at his side, he made his way toward the royal palace, where he found a great festival going on. On the throne, next to the king, sat a sad and weeping Danae. The king had taken advantage of Perseus's absence to force her to marry him. The wedding ceremony was just about to begin. Perseus had made it home just in time.

"Polydectes," he cried, "I am back, and I have brought you the gift I promised." Out of the bag at his side he pulled the bloody head of Medusa. Polydectes tried to scream, but his mouth froze. He had turned into solid rock. The head of Medusa was so terrifying that, even though she now was dead, she had not lost her power.

There was another guest at the party who became the victim of the Medusa. Perseus's grandfather, Acrisius, had been invited to the wedding. He and Polydectes were fast friends, since their characters were similar, and he had agreed to his daughter's marriage, in spite of her objections, because her future bridegroom had promised he would kill any sons she might have.

When his grandson Perseus held up the head of the Medusa, Acrisius also looked at it, and he, too, turned to stone. Danae told her son that this development had been prophesied by the Delphic Oracle, and that therefore he need not feel guilty at having killed his grandfather. It was a fate that had been decided by the gods even before Perseus was born.*

The people of the island were delighted to see Perseus again. It turned out that the fisherman who had rescued him from the sea was a remote relative of the dead king, and the only relative living. So the humble Dictys became the ruler of the kingdom, and, since he was much more intelligent and generous than Polydectes, he made all of his subjects happy and prosperous. After his death, Perseus became the king.

Perseus built a temple to Zeus and Hermes, and gave back all the magical gifts they had sent him so that from then on he would have to be clever and brave without supernatural help. The shield held the image of the Medusa head burned into it forever, and Athena kept it among her treasures.

Andromeda and Perseus got married and lived happily ever after. It is even possible that since he was the son of Zeus and she one of the most beautiful women in the world, they both went to the Elysian

---

* In another version of the story, Perseus takes part in a discus-throwing contest while the guest of a king in another country. Among the other guests, without Perseus's knowledge, is his grandfather. As he throws his discus, Zeus, who has been angry at Acrisius for the mistreatment of Danae, shifts the wind, so that the heavy object turns and hits Acrisius in the head, killing him instantly. In that way, the prophecy has also been fulfilled, and Perseus is not at fault for killing his grandfather.

Fields instead of Hades when it came time for them to leave the earth.

Chapter 21

Hercules: The Strongest Man on Earth

SOURCES: Most of the stories about the heroic deeds of Hercules come from folktale sources. Apollodorus, a prose writer of the second century A.D., wrote some of these stories down. Tales of the hero's earliest childhood are preserved in the works of two earlier poets, Pindar and Theocritus.

The fairy-tale–like adventures of Hercules turn into dark tragedy in the stories about his later life, however. These are best preserved in the plays of Sophocles and Euripides. The Roman poet Ovid also told of some of Hercules' early heroic deeds, but he, too, concentrated on the later tragedy.

One of the most persistent myths, that Hercules freed Prometheus from his unjust imprisonment and torture by Zeus and became a god himself, rising to Olympus along with the Titan he saved, seems to have no specific individual source. It may be the one way that some wandering unknown poets and tellers of tales *wanted* the story to end. It gives them a kind of glory that many Greeks apparently felt both Hercules and Prometheus deserved as their final destiny.

THE STORY: Hercules was born in Thebes, where most thought that he was the son of Amphitryon, a great general, and the general's wife, Alcmena. Actually, he was a son of Zeus, who had visited Alcmena disguised as her husband when the general was away at war. Alcmena had another son, Iphicles, who was Hercules' half-brother (his father *really* was Amphitryon). The difference in the two boys became evident when they were tiny babies. Hercules was strong, vital, and already brave. His half-brother was weak and cowardly. Hera, who had been watching Alcmena carefully, soon realized that Zeus was Hercules' father. Jealous as always, she determined to kill the child while he was still too young to defend himself.

One night after Alcmena had put the two little boys to bed, Hera sent two gigantic snakes to their room. As the snakes reared themselves to strike the babies with their venom or to wind themselves around their bodies to suffocate them, both children woke up. Iphicles screamed in terror and tried to flee. But Hercules grasped both snakes by the throat, one in each hand. They twisted and turned, and tried to bite him or to coil themselves around his little body, but he was already too strong for them. When his terrified father and mother rushed into the nursery, they found one son cowering in a corner and the other triumphantly holding up the bodies of two dead monsters.

It became evident, not only to his parents but to all who knew him, that Hercules was destined to become a great hero. Teiresias, one of the most respected prophets of Thebes, told his mother that the Greeks would eventually sing of his great deeds forever, and that he would become one of the legendary figures of all time.

Obviously, since they had a child with so much promise, his parents made sure that he received a first-rate education. He proved to be superb at all the skills taught in what we might today call "gym" or "physical education." Almost from the beginning he was able to win contests with some of the best teachers in Thebes in fencing, wrestling, driving a chariot, riding, and weight lifting. But he was not fond of what might be called "academic subjects." He particularly hated making music, a skill every educated person was thought to need. One day he hit his music teacher over the head with a lyre, killing the poor man. The death was, of course, unintentional, and Hercules was terribly sorry when he found out what he had done. He just did not know his own strength. Also, he had a terrible temper. His rages came suddenly, and left just as quickly, but in combination with his awesome strength, they led him to do terrible deeds.

When he managed to control himself, his accomplishments were great. By the time he was eighteen years old, he had already killed the Thespian lion, which roamed the countryside, terrifying the villagers and attacking their cattle and their children. He did not even use a weapon; he simply strangled the fierce animal to death. Ever after he wore its skin as a cloak, with the head forming a kind of hood over his own head. This is the way he is pictured in many vase paintings found in Thebes by modern archaeologists. Scholars may have had trouble recognizing other Greek heroes fighting a fierce animal or giant, but Hercules can always be identified by that lion's pelt.

A few years later, he fought and conquered (apparently by himself —no army is ever mentioned) the Minyans, a tribe that had been exacting tribute from Thebes for several generations. In gratitude, he was given the most beautiful maiden in the kingdom, Princess Megara, as his wife. She bore him three sons. The marriage was a very happy one; he loved her and his children, and even stayed home and refrained from attempting any more special adventures and heroic deeds.

However, Hera still hated him and could not bear to see him so happy. So, disguised as a sorceress, she gave him a potion that drove him insane. In his madness he killed his children, mistaking them for dangerous snakes; and when his wife, their mother, tried to protect her youngest child, he killed her, too. Then Hera took the cloak of madness away, and he saw what he had done.

He had no idea who was responsible. It seemed to him that one moment they had all been sitting together having a family meal, the next there were the bodies, bloodied and dead. He looked around and saw a large crowd of horrified servants.

"Who could have done such an awful thing?" he cried out. "Tell me who committed this terrible crime, so I can avenge my beloved wife and my poor babies." Nobody dared to answer him. They feared that in a rage he would kill anyone who told the truth. Finally his father, Amphitryon, approached him, because he knew that if Hercules did not find out who was responsible he might massacre everyone around. "You murdered your wife and sons," he said. "You suddenly went mad, and you are so strong that nobody could stop you, although everyone wanted to."

"So I am the one on whom I will have to avenge myself," Hercules cried out. He ran from the room, intending to kill himself. No gods or miracles saved him this time. Instead, his old friend Theseus (see Chapter 22), who happened to be in Thebes, came and stretched out his hands to him. The blood on Hercules' hands now also stained those of Theseus, and, according to ancient Greek belief, along with the blood, he had taken on himself some of his friend's guilt. Theseus persuaded Hercules that suicide was a coward's way out of sorrow.

"A real man bears his grief and his guilt, and tries to make amends for it," he said. (Theseus, unlike Hercules, was wise and sensitive as well as brave and strong.) "Come to Athens with me, and we will try to help you live through this tragedy." During the many days and nights Hercules spent with Theseus, he tried to explain that a man who has been driven mad by the gods is not responsible for his actions.

Hercules only half-believed Theseus. He still felt that he had to do something special to atone for the deaths of his wife and children. So, like many before him, he went to visit the Oracle at Delphi, and the priestess there tended to agree that he was defiled by his acts, and that he would not be clean again until he had paid a fearsome penance. To assign his punishment, she sent him to his cousin, Eurystheus, the king of Mycenae. Hercules thought that his cousin would order him tortured and killed, but Eurystheus was a practical person. He decided to use the powers of Hercules to rid the world of a number of dangers and nuisances that nobody else had been able to remove.

He gave Hercules twelve tasks, each considered all but impossible. These tasks became known as the "Labors Of Hercules."

The first task was to kill the lion of Nemea, a monstrous animal that roamed the countryside at will, terrifying and killing men and domestic animals alike. No one had been able to touch the lion because no weapon could even scratch it. Hercules, of course, had had experience with killing a lion before. He choked the animal to death, heaved its huge body on his shoulders, and carried it back into Mycenae. The king was delighted that the lion was dead, but also feared the enormous strength of Hercules and the danger it might represent. He would not allow his cousin to come back into the city, but made him set up camp outside, and sent messengers to assign the other tasks.

The second task was to go to a place called Lerna to kill a monster with nine heads, the Hydra. This was a harder labor than it seemed at first. One of the heads of the Hydra was immortal. The other eight might as well have been: Every time one of them got lopped off, two more grew in its place. This time Hercules took along an assistant, his nephew Iolaus. He asked the young man to hand him a burning torch every time he chopped off a head, and he seared the neck so that new heads could not sprout. As he removed each head, he buried it under a huge rock so that it could not harm anyone.

The third task was to bring back alive a hind, with golden horns like a stag, which was believed to be sacred to Artemis. Killing the animal would have been easy, but would have brought on Hercules the eternal enmity of Artemis. Hercules chased the stag for an entire year. Then finally he either stopped the creature by pinning its two front legs together with a well-shot arrow or caught it in a net and brought it back to his cousin. Artemis was angry at this, but Hercules explained why he had done it, and she forgave him.

His fourth task was to capture a huge wild boar, which was almost as terrifying as the lion of Nemea had been. This animal, too, could not be injured by any weapon. So Hercules chased the beast until it was exhausted, drove it into the deep snow, trapped it, and brought it back so it could be caged forever.

The fifth task was to clean the filthiest place on earth, the Augean stables. Augeas, a powerful warlord, had thousands of cattle, but he was lazy, and apparently did not mind the dirt and the stink these animals created. At any rate, the stables had never been cleaned. Hercules agreed to remove this environmental hazard in *one day*, alone—without any help. He diverted two rivers to run through the stables, and all the filth was washed away within minutes.

His sixth task was to drive away an enormous flock of birds, which were such a plague that the area around the marsh where they built their nests was uninhabitable. All the villagers and peasants had fled their homes to get away from the birds, which killed their cattle, carried away their children, and made life generally unbearable. This time Hercules had help. Since he could not walk into the marsh without drowning, nor sail a boat through its reeds, Athena gave him a rattle, which when shaken made such a noise that all the birds flew out of their nests into the air. As they flew away, Hercules was able to shoot them with his bow and arrow. In one day, he shot hundreds of thousands of birds, and the people who lived in the area could return to their homes.

The seventh task was to go to Crete and bring back a savage bull that Poseidon had given to the king, Minos. Again he was asked to bring the animal back alive, so as not to anger Poseidon. Hercules wrestled the bull down to earth, hog-tied him, put him on a boat, and brought him back to his cousin.

The eighth task was to bring back the man-eating mares that belonged to the ruler of a nearby kingdom. This king, who was called Diomedes, was very proud of these animals, and generally fed them the men, women, and children he had captured in wars. Hercules killed Diomedes, and drove back the mares to his cousin's kingdom. Apparently he so frightened the animals that they no longer wished to eat humans; instead they began to eat grass and hay, just like all other horses. Eurytheus dedicated them to Hera, who didn't want anything that had to do with Hercules. So they were simply turned loose on Mount Olympus.

The ninth task was to bring back the girdle of Hippolyta, the queen of the Amazons, a group of women warriors. The queen was very taken with Hercules, so she kindly agreed to give him her girdle without a fight. But Hera was on the scene to make trouble again. She disguised herself as an Amazon and told the rest of the Amazon army that Hercules had come to kidnap their queen. So the women charged his ship. Hercules, in his usual thoughtless fashion, immediately assumed that Hippolyta had ordered the attack, and killed her. Then he fought off the other women and departed with the girdle. This part of the myth is somewhat confusing, since, in another story, Theseus marries Hippolyta and takes her to Athens. Apparently, those who told the tales of Hercules were not familiar with the story about Theseus. This frequently happens when folktales about the same people are told in different parts of a country.

The tenth task was to find and bring to Mycenae the cattle of Geryon, said to be the strongest man alive. He had three heads, six hands, and three bodies, joined at the waist, and was king of an area in what is now in or near western Spain. On his way there, Hercules reached the land at the end of the Mediterranean. As a memorial of his journey, he set up two great rocks, then called the Pillars of Hercules (now they are Gibraltar and Ceuta). He killed the king and drove the cattle back to Mycenae.

The eleventh task sounded difficult even to Hercules. He was asked to bring back the Golden Apples of the Hesperides. The apples belonged to Hera, but were guarded by the Hesperides, the daughters of Atlas. Atlas was forced to carry the vault of heavens on his shoulders as punishment for fighting on the side of Cronus, Zeus's father during the war of the gods. Nevertheless, Hercules was advised to have Atlas get the apples for him.

Hercules went to Atlas and offered to carry his heavy burden while he went to get the apples. Just the thought of getting rid of that enormous load was enough to persuade Atlas to agree to Hercules' request. He went to get the apples, but on the way back he decided that he would not resume his position as carrier of the universe. He would simply leave Hercules to do that painful job. So he told Hercules that *he* would carry the apples to Eurystheus, and leave Hercules, who was strong enough for the task, to hold up the vaults of heaven. This time Hercules had to use his wits rather than his fists to accomplish his task. He succeeded only because Atlas, although as strong as Hercules, was less intelligent. When Hercules asked him to take over the burden of the heavens for just a minute so he could put pads on his shoulders, the Titan complied. Hercules laughed and ran away with the apples, leaving Atlas just where he had found him. The apples, incidently, eventually found their way back to the Hesperides because no one to whom they were given wanted to offend Hera by keeping them.

The twelfth and last task was the worst of all. Hera herself had thought it up, and suggested it to Eurystheus. Hercules was asked to go to Hades and bring back Cerberus, the three-headed dog who guarded Hades' gates. He was not allowed to use any weapons, and had to count entirely on his physical strength and the agility of his body. While looking for the monster in Hades, he came across his friend Theseus, who had gone to the land of the dead with a friend who wished to bring back someone he loved. Hercules rescued Theseus from the Seat of Forgetfulness, where the lord of Hades had imprisoned him, and sent him back to the land of the living. Then he wrestled the dreadful dog to the ground, tied him up, and brought him back to earth, turning him over to Eurystheus. This turned out to be one animal Eurystheus decided was too dangerous even for his zoo. He sent the dog back to Hades, where he belonged.

Hercules was now free from the taint of murder. But apparently he still had not learned to govern his temper or to recognize that there were other ways to settle disputes besides fighting real and imagined enemies to the death. For instance, Hercules fought a fierce battle with a river god for the love of a young woman, even though the god was perfectly willing to negotiate the matter. The god turned himself into a bull and attacked Hercules, who had no trouble subduing him and breaking off one of his horns. Hercules won the fight, and married the woman, Deianira, but he forgot that gods have excellent memories and powerful friends on Olympus, and that they never forgot a slight.

He killed, with a thrust of his mighty arm, accidentally again, a young boy who was serving him water at a feast. The boy's father forgave him, but Hercules did not forgive himself and went into exile for many years.

Later he deliberately killed a young man who was his guest because he believed that this man's father had insulted him. This killing was too much even for his father, Zeus, who punished him by sending him into a country ruled by Queen Omphale, who was one of Zeus's current favorites. She made the mighty Hercules dress like a woman and join her serving maids to do women's work, weaving and spinning. Because the punishment had been ordered specifically by Zeus, Hercules had to submit, but he felt shamed and degraded. He swore that as soon as he was free he would kill the young man's father, King Eurytus, whom he, quite unreasonably, held responsible for the punishment.

As soon as Zeus allowed Hercules to leave, he collected an army, attacked and captured the city of King Eurytus, and personally put him to death.

Apparently at this point, Zeus decided the time had come to remove the deadly Hercules from the earth. So he began to plot his end.

While Hercules was destroying the city of King Eurytus, he captured the daughter of Eurytus, Iole, and fell in love with her. Never tactful, he sent her home to wait for him until he had done a few more heroic deeds. Hercules' loving and loyal wife, Deianira, was not too surprised. Greek husbands, especially heroes, seldom seemed to be faithful. But Deianira did want to retain her husband's love. And she thought that she had a love potion strong enough to bring her wandering husband's affections back to her.

It seems that while she and Hercules were on their honeymoon, they had met with a Centaur, who carried the bride off to the middle of a river and tried to rape her. She cried out in terror, and Hercules, from the shore, shot the creature with one of his arrows. As the Centaur was bleeding to death, he asked Deianira to catch some of his blood in a bottle she was carrying. "I love you so much, and I am so sorry for what I tried to do to you that I want to be sure your husband loves you forever," he told her. "So, to make up for my sin, I will now tell you that my blood is the strongest love potion in the universe. If you ever feel that you are in danger of losing Hercules, just touch him with this blood, and his love will immediately return to you."

But the blood was not a love potion; it was deadly poison. When Deianira anointed a beautiful robe with it and sent it to Hercules, he, of course, put it on. And almost at once he became deathly ill. He rolled on the floor in agony. He tried to cool his burning body by leaping into the ocean. Nothing worked. Unfortunately he was half immortal, and he could not die.

When word came to Deianira of what she had done, she committed suicide. Hercules, by his thoughtlessness, had indirectly killed yet another person whom he loved, and who loved him. He desperately wished for his own death, but the poison only made him sicker with every day that passed.

Finally, he ordered his servants to build a huge funeral pyre on Mount Aetna, and to carry him there. Hercules knew, because Zeus had told him so in a dream, that the mighty fire that would be lighted under him would finally end his agony on earth. He asked one of his young archers to shoot a flaming arrow into the wood pyre. But Hercules had disappeared even before the fire started to burn. The gods had lifted him bodily from this earth to Mount Olympus, where, as the son of Zeus, he would be allowed to remain for all eternity, or as long as the gods of Olympus ruled.

According to some legends, he even reconciled with Hera and married one of her daughters.

Chapter 22

Theseus: The Favorite Hero

of Athens

SOURCES: Theseus appears as a minor character in many early Greek legends. Usually there is a reference to some of his heroic and extraordinary deeds, and then the story goes on to tell about another god, hero, or villain. Many experts believe that there was an early version of the Theseus story that is now lost, but there is no doubt that stories about him were told by poets who went from festival to festival, singing or reciting their tales.

From the early references we have, it is obvious that the Athenians considered him their special hero. He was described as relatively small in stature, yet enormously strong and clever. Apparently he practiced an early kind of karate, and he used his relatively small size to overcome much larger, more powerful opponents through special skills. This must have pleased the citizens of Athens, which, compared to some other city-states, was also relatively small. They also respected brains more than brawn.

Theseus appears, not as a main character, in plays by Euripides and Sophocles. Theseus's entire story comes to us in the writings of the Roman writer Ovid and the Greek Apollodorus.

The entire tale, collected from its many sources, emerges as a rather strange mix of fairy tale and tragedy. Up to a point, the life of Theseus is much like the life of Perseus. From an obscure and poverty-stricken childhood, hidden away from possible harm, he moves to a brilliant young manhood with a long unbroken string of victories over terrible mythical monsters and a triumphant homecoming to a cheering Athens.

This all seems to belong to oral tradition, to tales told by the wandering poets. But when the Greek dramatists took over, the history of Theseus darkened immediately. Eventually, he is overtaken by an evil fate, just as most of the other heroes whose stories pass out of the simple folktale phase into the written work of great poets and playwrights. So, in the end, we have *two* stories: one a bright fairy tale and the other a dark tragedy.

Today in Athens and in the Greek countryside, the character of Theseus as he appears in the early stories is the one that is heard most often. Indeed, there seem to be some who think of Theseus as two people: the one their mothers and grandmothers told them about when they were children, and the one they see when they visit one of the ancient theaters for the plays by Sophocles and Euripides.

THE STORY: As a child, Theseus lived with his mother in a small hut near the sea. Often he listened with astonishment when his mother told him that he was actually the son of a king and might

1 0 1

become a ruler of a great city when he was grown. She never told him who his father was, but he had heard the villagers whisper two stories. One was that his father was the king of Athens, Aegeus, who had ordered his mother to keep him hidden because his uncle and cousins wanted to take over the kingdom and might have him killed. The other story was that his father was actually the sea god, Poseidon, who would eventually make sure that Theseus inherited his rightful place: the throne of Athens.

Theseus was rather small, although wiry and strong, so the village bullies often attacked him and made his life miserable.

To survive, he exercised constantly, running, lifting heavy rocks, and swimming in the sea against strong tides and high waves. But the large bullies in his village still often succeeded in beating him in the fights they provoked. One day, when he had been severely beaten by the largest village bully, he went down to the sea to rest on a rock. He might have fallen asleep for a while, but he suddenly woke up as he heard a voice that seemed to come from the depth of the ocean.

"Being small is not the same as being weak," the voice said. "Let me give you a riddle."

"What's a riddle got to do with winning battles with bullies?" Theseus wanted to know.

"This one does," the voice answered. "Have you ever wondered why gulls can crack big sea clams open, but cannot crack shrimps or scallops? The answer is that the size of the clams makes them vulnerable and stiff. Shrimps and scallops are too light. They use their smallness to defeat their enemies. You can use the same method. Don't fight on the large bullies' terms, fight on your own. Use your speed and agility to force your bigger and slower attacker to throw *himself* off balance. When he is wavering, you've got him."

"Whose voice are you?" Theseus asked.

"I don't want to tell you that," the voice said. "I may just be a very clever sea gull, or I may be Poseidon; but whoever I am, the principle works. Just try it."

So, on his way home, when Theseus was attacked, as usual, by one of the largest bullies in the village, Theseus allowed the boy to thrust out his fist. Then he grabbed him around the wrist and pulled him further into the direction of the thrust. The bigger boy lost his balance, and Theseus tossed him over his left shoulder. The boy was almost as angry as he was astonished, so he tried to kick Theseus in the leg with his foot. Theseus grabbed the boy's ankle and tossed him over his right shoulder. This time the attacker gave up and ran away.

From then on, Theseus was always able to use a bigger and stronger opponent's own body weight and clumsy motion to defeat him. Someone had taught him a fighting method that in the Orient is now known as karate.

The bullies not only left him alone, they began to respect him, and, in time, he became a village leader.

Now it was true that Aegeus could have been the father of Theseus. And he knew it. Though he had gone to Athens before the boy was born, he had left a sword and a pair of sandals under a heavy rock. When the boy who was to be born could move the rock and rescue the sword and sandals, Aegeus said, he should come to Athens. So one day when Theseus became a young man, he moved the rock with no difficulty, and removed the sword and sandals. Clearly it was time for him to go to Athens.

The easiest way to make the journey was by ship. But Theseus did not want to take the easy way. He insisted on going overland, a long and dangerous route. In fact, the road from his village to Athens was known as the most dangerous in Greece. It was infested with cruel bandits who killed travelers in terrible ways, with giants, with monsters, and with other mysterious beings known for their cruelty and bloodlust. Usually travelers who had to go to Athens by land moved in large groups, so as to better defend themselves. But Theseus insisted that he would go alone, to prove, once and for all, his bravery, cleverness, and fighting ability.

The first unknown persons he met, at the fork of a road, seemed harmless enough. They were two women: one dressed simply in a white flowing gown with her hair in shining strands down her back, the other dressed in sumptuous silks and jewels with her hair done in elaborate braids and curls. Since Theseus did not know the way to Athens, he asked the two women which road he should take.

"Follow me," said the beautiful, bejeweled one. "If you follow me, you will have an easy, rich life, with untold wealth, wonderful food, and all the beautiful women you might desire. My name is Pleasure."

"Follow your own good sense, always consulting the stars, the winds, and other natural signposts, and you will get where you want to go," the other said. "I can't promise you an easy life, just a useful one. My name is Wisdom."

"I never wanted an easy life. That's for weaklings, not heroes," said Theseus. He knew that Athens was due north, so he politely bade the two women good-bye, and started north, following the advice of Wisdom.

Next he met a huge man, twice his size, carrying an enormous club. The man reached out a hairy hand and seized Theseus by the throat while lifting the club over the young man's head.

"Who are you, and what do you want?" asked Theseus.

"I am Corynetes, known as the Cudgeler," the giant said. "I hate travelers to intrude into my territory, and I mean to use my cudgel to beat your brains out."

Using all his skill, Theseus grabbed the giant's wrist with one hand and picked up the cudgel that the surprised attacker dropped with the other. He hit the Cudgeler over the head with all his strength, cracking his skull open.

"Serves him right," said Theseus. "From now on I will punish every thief, brigand, and monster who attacks me in exactly the same way that he has used on his victims. An eye for an eye."

The next brigand he met was another large, ugly man who carried a gleaming battle-ax as big as a medium-sized tree. "Everyone who passes here washes my feet," the ax-bearer said. Theseus had heard of him. While travelers were busy washing his feet, he always chopped off their heads and fed them to his ever-hungry, oversized turtle. The ax-bearer was called Sciron, and the turtle, a man-eating monster, usually swam in the ocean under a cliff over which Sciron would kick his dead, headless victims.

When Sciron made his request, Theseus pretended to comply.

He knelt down and waited for the ax-bearer to lift his foot off the ground. Sciron always kicked his victims in the stomach so that they would fall over backward and he could cut off their heads. But this time Sciron got a surprise. When the foot came up, Theseus took hold of it and gave it a mighty tug. It was the ax-bearer who lost his balance and fell, dropping his weapon. Theseus picked up the ax, cut off Sciron's head, and pushed his body into the sea. The turtle was not very particular. He ate his master, just as he had previously swallowed his master's victims.

The next villain Theseus met was called Sinis. He was a robber who made sure that none of those whose money and property he took were left alive to tell their story. His technique was to press a pine tree to the ground. Then he would tell the visitor to hold it for a moment while he went to fetch a cool drink. Most travelers were too frightened to say no, and would grasp the top of the tree. Then Sinis would let go, and the tree would snap upright, flinging the traveler high into the air. He would dangle on the tree as long as he could, but eventually he would fall and be killed as he hit the ground. Theseus, however, knew exactly how to distribute his weight and was able to hold the top of the tree down. The robber, astounded that his usual method of disposing of travelers was not working, came closer to see what had gone wrong. As he stood over the tree, Theseus suddenly let it go, and it snapped back, hitting the robber in the head. He dropped to the ground, unconscious.

Theseus then bent down two trees a few feet apart. He tied one of the bandit's arms and one of his legs to one tree, and the other arm and leg to the other. Then he let both trees snap back. Half of the robber was left on one of the trees, the rest of him on the other. He would never again kill an innocent traveler on the way to Athens.

Theseus, who by now had had a difficult day, decided to look for a cottage where he might spend a restful night. He found a small house that, according to the sign in front, was an inn for weary travelers. There were lights inside, and he could spot fire in the grate. It all looked very cozy, but the inn turned out to be another trap. Many poor travelers, who had somehow managed to avoid the bandits Theseus had already defeated, had been killed there.

The hut belonged to a thief called Procrustes, who invited his guest inside. In the one room he saw a bed with bolts and leather bindings.

"When you lie down, I am going to make sure that you get your proper rest, so I will tie you down," the host said. "And to make sure that you are comfortable, I will see to it that you are exactly the right size for this bed. If you are too long, I will chop off your legs and make you fit. And if you are too short, I will turn the bed into a machine that will stretch you until you are tall enough for it."

"You can't think that I would be crazy enough to get into this bed myself," Theseus said. "You'll have to make me lie down."

"No problem, that's easy," said his host, as he put his huge hand on Theseus's chest to push him down. Theseus, however, took hold of the man's wrist and flung him over his shoulder right onto the bed. There he tied him down, turned on the stretching machine, and left. Procrustes' screams could be heard for miles, but there was, of course, no one about to save him.

Theseus decided that he had had enough adventures, and would walk straight to Athens, avoiding any more places where monsters and robbers might be waiting for him. When he arrived, news of his great deeds had preceded him. He showed the king, Aegeus, the sword he had taken from under the stone, and the king was delighted to see that the young man he considered to be his son was so brave, strong, and handsome. But Theseus noticed that in spite of his joy, he often turned his head away and looked sadly out of a window, watching a procession led by seven of the most beautiful maidens and seven of the handsomest young men he had ever seen. And it was not only the king who was sad. Wailing and crying came from every direction. It seemed as if all of Athens was in mourning.

"What is happening, King Aegeus?" Theseus asked. "Why is everyone so unhappy?"

"It's a short, sad story," Aegeus said. "A few years ago we were defeated in a war by the island of Crete. The king of Crete, Minos, is a very cruel man. He has told us that if we don't provide him with seven of our most beautiful young girls and seven of our most handsome young men every year to sacrifice to a monster he keeps on the island, he will attack us. Should that happen, probably all of us would be killed by his soldiers and by the horrible monster called the Minotaur, which is half-man and half-bull. There is a rumor that the Minotaur is actually the son of King Minos's mad wife, and that his father was the strongest, largest bull in the universe. This terrible being requires human flesh to eat, and once a year we have to provide the human sacrifice. Today is the day that our young men and women have to board the ship to Crete to be sacrificed to the Minotaur."

"I think the gods sent me to Athens to put a stop to this terrible custom," Theseus said. "Send me instead one of the other young men who has been selected for this year. I will go to Crete and take care of the Minotaur and King Minos. When I have killed the Minotaur, I will bring all those Athenian young people back with me. Poseidon will protect me, and it will give me great pleasure to free you and your people forever from this curse."

King Aegeus, realizing that his son would not be stopped, embraced him and said that he would pray to Poseidon every day to keep Theseus safe. "I will be waiting for you. Every day I will go to the shore to watch for your returning ship," he said. "Please ask the sailors to change the black sails, with which you will be departing for Crete, to white sails, if you and the other young Athenians are safe." Theseus promised to remember this request, and left.

When the ship docked at Crete, almost the whole population of the capital city, Knossos, was waiting at the harbor, shouting and having fun. The day the human sacrifices arrived from Athens was always a festival day. The Athenians were marched through the crowd to the palace to meet King Minos, who had to approve each one as being beautiful or handsome enough to meet the requirements of the sacrificial ritual.

In the king's throne room, Theseus stepped forward. "I am the only son of the king of Athens," he said, "and I, therefore, ask for a privilege: I want to meet the Minotaur first, by myself. I think this is due my rank." Minos was astonished. Usually the Athenians showed no eagerness at all to meet the monster that would eat them.

Behind the king stood his two daughters, Ariadne and Phaedra, who admired the courage of the young man. They had never met anyone quite like him. Not only was he good-looking, but he carried himself not like a victim but like a prince. Ariadne immediately fell in love with him. Of course, she did not know that Poseidon had asked Aphrodite, as a special favor, to make Theseus irresistible to her, and that she was entirely in the power of the goddess of love.

Minos, on the other hand, thought it might be amusing to send this cocky young man to his doom all by himself, to be followed later by his companions. So he agreed to the request. Meanwhile, all the Athenians were locked up in the palace cellar for the night. Theseus, because he was a prince, got a cell by himself at the suggestion of Ariadne.

Just before dawn, when Theseus was to be led to the Minotaur, Ariadne arrived at his cell. "I love you," she told the young man. "And I will save you, even if that means I have to betray my father and my people. Listen carefully. The Minotaur is kept in a labyrinth: rows and rows of dense hedges making up thousands of lanes. Most lead to the center, where the monster has his lair. There is only *one* lane out, and nobody ever has been able to find it. So the Minotaur's victims have two impossible choices: They can stand still and wait for the monster to come to them, or they can walk further and further into the labyrinth, until they walk into the monster's lair. Either way, he devours them. But I know of a trick that will help you to get out. The architect my father forced to build the labyrinth taught it to me."

She pulled out of her pocket a very large ball of shiny yellow silk twine. "The architect said that this twine is long enough to lead you to the monster's lair. So you must tie one end to the entrance doorpost, and then slowly unwind the silk. If you kill the Minotaur, as you say you can, you will be able to follow the thread back to the entrance and get out. After you are out, I will make sure that you and your friends get back to Athens. Leave that to me. But I want you to promise that you will take me back with you and marry me." Theseus promised that he would marry the young princess, and she handed him the silk.

A few minutes later the king's soldiers came to take him to the labyrinth. Theseus went quietly, not boasting that he would kill the monster (that would have been hubris) and not crying out for mercy (that would have been cowardice). When he had been led to the gate of the labyrinth and told to walk on, he waited until the soldiers looked another way, then carefully tied one end of the silk twine to a bush. As he walked, he allowed the bright yellow thread to unravel behind him, knowing that it would lead him back to the entrance.

There are several versions of the way Theseus found and killed the Minotaur, which was not just half-man and half-bull. He was also a giant. His huge, well-muscled bull's body was covered with dark matted hair. His head had small red eyes, a huge mouth, slobbering spit and blood, and sharp, shiny horns, as large as elephants' tusks. Theseus had no weapons to overcome this horrible monster. So, according to one story, he killed it with his fists as the half-human, half-animal being slept.

The other story is much more astounding and heroic. Theseus again used his skills of weights and balances to overcome the Minotaur. As the animal charged him, howling and growling, Theseus took hold of one of the horns and swung himself on top of the animal's head. There he held onto both horns and could not be dislodged, no matter how hard the monster tried to shake him off. While there, he dug his heels into the monster's eyes to blind him.

The Minotaur, being half-man, had hands as well as four legs with hooves. When he tried to use one gigantic fist to pull Theseus off and crush him to death, Theseus, using both his arms, held the wrist tightly, and swung himself over the Minotaur's back to the ground. The monster lost its balance briefly and fell. Now Theseus took hold of one horn, twisted it with all his might, and every time the monster tried to turn his head to shake off the young man, Theseus would twist in the opposite direction, thus turning the monster's very strength against itself, as he had learned from the voice on the beach (which might have been that of Poseidon).

In the struggle, he finally broke off the horn. The monster, mad with pain and half-blinded, attacked Theseus again. Theseus used the sharp horn like a dagger to parry and thrust. The monster kept trying to pin Theseus against the side of the labyrinth. Theseus, small and agile, was always able to escape. As the Minotaur got more tired, he became increasingly careless. Finally, with Theseus behind him, stabbing his back with the horn, the monster turned around and ran at his enemy. Theseus was ready. Holding the horn steady, he allowed the Minotaur to run into it. It plunged deep into the creature's forehead.

The Minotaur gave one terrible shriek and died. Theseus took off the other horn and, following the bright yellow thread, found his way out of the labyrinth, where a crowd of local citizens came running toward him. Some were upset that the Minotaur was dead and that the annual human sacrifice festival was now over forever. But many others were delighted. They had long realized that a terrible weapon like the Minotaur could devastate their enemies, but it also might turn or be turned against them. So they were relieved to see the monster dead.

King Minos realized that for much of his population Theseus had become a popular hero. Popular heroes have been known to overthrow unpopular kings, so he was only too pleased to let the young prince go. Ariadne begged to be allowed to go with him, to marry him, and Phaedra said she wanted to be with her sister. So the king allowed both of his daughters to depart for Athens, along with Theseus and the other would-be Athenian sacrificial victims.

On the way, the ship landed on an island called Naxos to take on provisions. What happened there is reported in two different ways. According to one story, Theseus had decided that he was in love with Phaedra, so he just deserted Ariadne on the island and sailed away. According to the other story, he was on the boat, working on the sails, when a violent storm arose and carried the ship out to sea. When, after weeks of struggling with wind and tides, he was able to return to Naxos, Ariadne, who only *thought* that she had been deserted, had died of grief. Athenians, who love the Theseus legend, prefer to believe the second version. At any rate, Theseus married Phaedra.

The ship sailed toward Athens, carrying the young prince and the Athenian men and women who had been selected to become the victims of the Minotaur. Everyone was excited at finally getting home safely. Theseus probably still had the problem of Ariadne on his mind. In any case, he forgot to order his sailors to change the black sails to white ones, as he had promised his father.

Meanwhile in Athens, King Aegeus had kept a faithful watch on the hill overlooking the sea. When he saw the ship on the horizon with its black sails, he became desperate.

"I am responsible for this tragedy," he cried. "I have sent my only son to certain death. I do not deserve to live." He got on his horse and rode off the cliff into the raging sea below. Ever since then that sea has borne his name: Aegean.

Theseus, of course, was exceedingly sorry that his mistake had caused his father's death. He spent many months mourning him. But Athens needed a ruler, so eventually he was crowned king. He ruled justly and well, and his subjects loved him. Indeed, even today, he is clearly the favorite hero of the Athenians.

This is where the folktale version of the Theseus story officially ends, although Theseus appears as a minor character in the stories of other Greek heroes, usually to show what a kindly and generous person he was. For instance, he received the elderly Oedipus (see Chapter 24) at his court when other kings shunned him, and was with him when he died. And when Hercules went mad and killed his wife and children (see Chapter 21), only Theseus, of all the people whom he had befriended, refused to abandon him.

But Theseus had one flaw. He loved adventure for its own sake, and instead of remaining quietly in Athens, enjoying his power and prosperity, he occasionally went to war for causes that were not really in his country's special interest. Usually he fought his battles on the side of those who were oppressed or had been wronged in some other way, however.

For instance, when the king of Thebes refused to bury the enemy dead who had been slaughtered in battles against that mighty country, Theseus led an army against Thebes. When he won, all that he required was that the dead of other wars should be honorably buried.

(The Greeks believed that unburied dead were forever doomed to roam the earth as tortured spirits, and therefore burial was exceedingly important to them.)

A little later he decided that he would go into the country of the Amazons, a place ruled by women warriors who were so strong and brave that they had never been defeated by any male army. He defeated their troops and took away with him their queen, whose name was Hippolyta or, some say, Antiope. Since he was already married to Phaedra, this was bound to cause complications, although some legends say he did not marry Phaedra until long after his association with Hippolyta. If this is not so, then Phaedra shared her husband and her throne with a fellow queen; but Hippolyta soon died, bearing a son, whom Theseus called Hippolytus. This child was sent to the country to be brought up in a peasant village, just as Theseus himself had been. Perhaps he feared that Phaedra might want to harm her rival's child. She did . . . but not until many years later.

The end of the Theseus story is a terrible tragedy. It is told in the drama *Hippolytus*, written by the playwright Euripides in 428 B.C. Apparently he had written another play about Theseus earlier, which is lost. According to many of today's experts, it was not a success, and may never have been shown in Athens. However, the play we have about Hippolytus, Theseus, and Phaedra was considered highly successful, and was performed many times, although to us, judging in light of today's moral values, it may seem more than a little confusing.

Euripides clearly indicated, by starting his story toward the end of the Theseus tale, that he expected his audience to know from other sources who the various characters in the play were.

The play begins when Hippolytus, now an exceedingly handsome and attractive young man, had returned from the country to the court of his father. He was admired by everyone for his bravery, his many military and artistic skills, and his purity of spirit. Sometime in the past Hippolytus had dedicated his life to the virgin goddess Artemis. He had vowed never to fall in love with a mortal woman, and never to marry. His attitude made Aphrodite furious. It seemed to her that the young man was afflicted with hubris.

So, while Theseus was away on one of his adventure trips, she asked her son Eros to wound Phaedra with his fatal arrow of love, and to make sure that the man with whom she fell in love was her stepson Hippolytus. Phaedra told Hippolytus how she felt, and tried to get him to make love to her. Hippolytus was more than shocked; he was revolted. He pushed her away in disgust and left the palace. Phaedra's love turned to hate and thoughts of revenge, but her hate was as much for herself as for the young man who had spurned her. She hanged herself, leaving a note accusing Hippolytus of raping her.

Just as her servingwomen were taking her body from her chamber into the main hall of the palace, Theseus returned and read the note. He went to find Hippolytus, who swore not only that he was innocent, but also boasted of his purity and his total commitment to Artemis. Again, under ancient Greek standards, he was exhibiting hubris. His father did not believe him. "My wife would not have committed suicide and left a note accusing you of this terrible crime if it were not true," he told his son. "I should kill you. But I will be merciful. I will only ban you from Athens. Get out of this city and never let me set eyes on you again." He also uttered a powerful curse, asking the gods to punish his son for his awful deed.

The curse soon took effect. Aphrodite persuaded Poseidon to raise a terrible monster from the sea. As Hippolytus rode along the shore, his horse, terrified by the monster, went wild and threw the young man violently to the ground. He was mortally wounded.

Meanwhile, Artemis had not remained inactive. She had gone to Theseus and told him the truth: that his son was completely innocent, and that his dead wife was a victim of Aphrodite's wiles.

Theseus followed Hippolytus to beg his forgiveness, but it was too late. When he reached his son, he saw him mortally wounded on the ground. Brokenhearted, Theseus threatened to commit suicide, but Artemis appeared again to comfort both father and son.

"This was not your fault, Theseus," she assured him. "It was Aphrodite playing one of her vicious games. Neither you nor Hippolytus will ever be forgotten as long as Greek art and history survive. You will both be remembered in song and story as virtuous, heroic men. You have the word of a goddess that both your names will be praised throughout eternity."

So, after his son died in his arms, Theseus sadly went back to his palace, which was now a lonely and desolate place. The Athenians were so horrified by the unjust banishment and death of Hippolytus that they took away Theseus's crown and banished him in turn.

He went to the court of an old friend, got into an argument, and was killed.

Meanwhile, the Athenians had reconsidered their harsh judgment when they learned that both Theseus and his son were really the victims of a feud between Artemis and Aphrodite, and that, therefore, what the two men had done was not their own fault. They had Theseus's body returned and built a great tomb for him, declaring that this site would forever be considered a sanctuary for slaves and others who were poor or persecuted, to honor the hero who throughout his life had fought on the side of the helpless and unprotected.

Chapter 23

The Golden Fleece, Jason, and Medea

SOURCES: The story of the Golden Fleece is one of those long, complicated folktales that appear in many civilizations. There seem to be endless variations, and new versions were apparently added many times through the centuries.

The story has its roots, apparently, in a number of preliterate poems and tales, which may actually have been told separately before being woven into one whole by the third-century B.C. poet Apollonius of Rhodes. He ends his poem with the return of the band of heroes who searched for the Golden Fleece and brought it back to Greece.

Apollonius tells the traditional folktale with the equally traditional happy ending. His Medea has magical powers, but she is what folktale scholars call a *white* witch, someone who uses witchcraft to combat evil and help the hero win his battles against the forces of darkness.

There are, however, indications that even in some folktales that preceded Apollonius, Medea was regarded as an evil witch. For instance, in one version of the Theseus story, she attempts to poison the young hero at a banquet given by his father, the king of Athens, but is discovered in time and makes her escape in a carriage drawn by two fire-spitting dragons. There are a number of other myths in which Medea appears as an evil presence, plotting the death of a hero or of a woman she hates. There is no record of what eventually happened to her. She may have been a semigoddess, and therefore an immortal evil being.

In Euripides' play *Medea,* she is neither a witch nor an evil spirit, but a person. Euripides' heroes and heroines are all mixtures of good and evil. He is nonjudgmental in his portrayal of his principal characters, who may commit horrendous deeds (Medea kills her two small children), but they are either driven to do them by uncontrollable emotions, or have reasons or beliefs that make their actions almost inevitable. In order to humanize Medea, Euripides also reinterpreted Jason. Instead of a shining young hero, he becomes a middle-aged, power-hungry, cruel man, who drives the woman who loves him to madness and murder.

THE STORY: The tale of the Golden Fleece begins long before the birth of Jason. Centuries earlier, sometime in the dark ages of Greece, when humans were still sacrificed to the gods, there lived a king called Athamas, who got tired of his first wife, Nephele, and replaced her with a younger, more beautiful woman, Princess Ino. Not only was Ino more attractive than the aging Nephele, she was also the daughter of a powerful king: Cadmus of Thebes. So, besides getting a more desirable wife, Athamas was also adding to the wealth and strength of his own realm through an alliance with a powerful father-in-law.

Nephele was afraid for her two children. She knew that her son, Phrixus, was the rightful heir to the throne, and she feared that his new stepmother would try to kill him. Unfortunately, she was right.

Princess Ino devised an elaborate plan. She got into the granary that held all the seed corn for the next harvest and parched it so that when it was sown it produced no corn. This left the country close to starvation. The king sent to the Oracle at Delphi for an explanation. Probably the priestess there told him the truth: that his beautiful new wife had spoiled the seed grain. But Ino was taking no chances. She had the messenger murdered, and substituted for him one of her own servants, who told the king that the gods were angry at him, and that he would not see another bountiful harvest until he sacrificed his little son, Phrixus.

The boy was torn from his mother's arms and taken to the sacrificial altar. But Nephele prayed for Zeus to save the child, and Zeus sent a ram with fleece of pure gold to take the boy away. The ram flew Phrixus to the country of Colchis, where he was put under the protection of its king. Eventually Phrixus sacrificed the ram to Zeus, giving the precious Golden Fleece to the king of Colchis.

Much later a whole other set of developments concerning the Golden Fleece began. An uncle of Jason, Pelias, stole the throne of Iolcus from his brother Aeson. Aeson was kept a prisoner, but his wife managed to send his young son, Jason, out of the country. She was sure that the wicked uncle would kill the boy to make sure that one of his own sons succeeded him on the throne.

Jason was reared by Chiron the Centaur, half man and half horse, on Mount Pelion, but from the time he was a very young child, he knew that he was the rightful ruler of Iolcus, and that someday he must overthrow the cruel king who had stolen the throne.

When Jason became eighteen years old, he decided that he was now mature enough to assume the rule of his kingdom. But, of course, his uncle was still very much in power in Iolcus. Jason was obviously somewhat unworldly. He certainly was not a master politician. He decided that the simplest, and therefore the best, course to take would be to go to Iolcus, announce that he was the real king, and simply ask his uncle to give him back the throne.

The wicked uncle had been waiting for him. He had been told by the Oracle at Delphi that he would die at the hands of a relative, and that he should beware of any man who wore just *one* sandal.

The day before Jason was to enter the city, the leather thongs that held his left sandal broke, and he could find nothing with which to repair them. So he came into the town, wearing just one sandal. He also wore peasant's clothes. But he was so handsome, with long, blond locks flowing down his back, strong muscular limbs, and a superb body, that many who saw him decided he must be a god in disguise: Apollo or Hermes, perhaps. So they sent for the king to find out who the stranger might be.

The king took one look at the handsome youth, noticed he was wearing only one sandal, and became terrified. There was also a strong family resemblance, and he suspected that this might be Jason, the rightful heir to the kingdom.

Since the crowd around the young man obviously admired him, Pelias did not dare do him any harm. In his friendliest voice, he offered him hospitality and asked him who he was, and where he came from. Jason's answer confirmed his worst fears. "I am your nephew, the son of the rightful ruler of this kingdom," he said. "I am therefore his heir, and the throne belongs to *me*. You may keep all the wealth you have acquired, but I plan to be the king of this country."

Pelias had to think quickly to find a way to answer Jason's claim. He had not been a popular ruler, and it was obvious that the crowd gathered around them believed the handsome youth. Even those who did not might want to exchange an aging ruler whom they disliked and feared for a young one who seemed to show so much promise.

So Pelias showed Jason his friendliest face and said, "You look as if you might be telling the truth. But, of course, we must have some kind of proof. Once an oracle told me that the man who would succeed me would bring the famous Golden Fleece of Phrixus, who is an ancestor of this family, back to Greece. If you can do this, I and my people will consider it a sign from Zeus that you are who you say you are, and that the throne of this country does indeed belong to you. I will then step down quietly and let you rule the country. I will even give you most of the wealth that I have acquired, and retire to the modest cottage where your father now lives.

Jason, like all of the Greek heroes, loved the idea of adventure. He knew, however, that he would need help to find the Golden Fleece and bring it back. So he issued a proclamation: He needed a group of brave and resourceful men to join him on his quest. The best and the brightest came to join him. Among them were many of the heroes of other Greek legends: the strong Hercules, Orpheus, the master musician, and Pelius, the father of the greatest Greek soldier in the Trojan War, Achilles (see Chapter 30). He also had the help of two powerful goddesses who usually managed to oppose each other. Both Hera and Athena were so enchanted with the young man that they entered into a pact to help him wherever and whenever they could.

So under the protection of the two mighty goddesses, the young heroes set sail on the ship *Argo* (they are sometimes called "the Argonauts"). Before pulling up anchor, they poured a glass of wine into the sea as a sacrifice to Zeus, and asked him to help speed them on their way. Zeus was impressed with their courage and initiative, and he, too, vowed that he would help them.

On the way they had a series of adventures that would have cost the lives of lesser men. First they came to the island of Lemnos, inhabited by women who had killed their husbands and now lived without men. Upon wise advice from an older woman in their midst, however, they welcomed the Argonauts, fell in love with them, and eventually allowed them to leave in peace, with water and food for their journey.

After another adventure in which they accidently killed a king who mistook them for pirates, the travelers lost one of their most valuable men. Hercules had a young armor-bearer of whom he was exceedingly fond. Hylas was a beautiful young boy, and a water nymph in a pond spotted him one night when the group was ashore getting supplies. She rose up out of the water and threw her arms around him to kiss him. Hylas was pulled down, and Hercules jumped into the water to rescue him. He could not find him, and was so disheartened by his loss that he decided to leave the expedition to continue his search for the boy. We don't know whether he ever found him.

After another adventure, in which another king was killed (his own fault, this time), the Argonauts found themselves on an island that was inhabited by the Harpies, terrible flying creatures with hooked claws and beaks, who not only stole all the food they could find, but who left behind them such a frightful stench that all living creatures around them became ill and died.

It so happened that on the beach where the Argonauts landed their ship, a helpless, miserable old man, a king actually, had pitched his tent. He was the victim of another of the many feuds between the gods. Apollo had admired him and rewarded him with the gift of prophecy; but the man had foretold the future so well that he angered Zeus, who, instead of taking his anger out on Apollo, decided to punish the old king. So he blinded him and sent the Harpies after him. Wherever he went, a swarm of Harpies circled over his head. And whenever he found something to eat, the Harpies would swoop down, gobble up most of the food, and defile the rest so that no one could bear to look at it or smell it, never mind eat it. By now the poor man had almost starved to death, and was crawling helplessly along the ground.

He begged Jason and his friends to help him. His gift of prophecy had told him that there were only two men on earth who would be able to free him from Zeus's curse, and they were among the Argonauts: the sons of Boreas, the Great North Wind. These two agreed to help.

They put some of their most delicious food on a plate before him, but of course, as soon as they set down the plate the Harpies appeared out of the sky and devoured everything, leaving a terrible stink behind. The two sons of the north wind were ready for them, however. They flew after the horrible animals and would have killed them with their swords if a messenger of the gods had not arrived just in time to tell them not to hurt the Harpies. They were, for some inexplicable reason, among Zeus's pets. The messenger, however, also said that Zeus had decided he had punished the old king enough, and from now on he would be allowed to eat his meals in peace. Since that was really what the Argonauts had in mind, they let the Harpies fly away, watched the old man enjoy a meal, and departed for their next adventure.

In gratitude, the old man had used his power of prophecy to keep them from another impending disaster. He told them that to get to their destination they would have to pass through the Clashing Rocks. These huge stones rolled perpetually, back and then against each other, crushing all ships that tried to pass. The way to get through these rocks, he said, was to first allow a dove to pass through. If the dove made it through safely, they too would do so. He even gave Jason a cage with a dove inside.

So, when the *Argo* came to the clashing rocks, Jason released the dove, which managed to pass between the stones, only losing a few tail feathers. As the stones opened, the rowers on the *Argo* worked with all their might, and the ship got through the rocks, with only a small ornament on the stern destroyed.

The Argonauts sailed past the rock on which Prometheus was bound hand and foot, with vultures eating away at his liver. But they did not stop. They had been warned that there was nothing they could do to help Prometheus. Another hero (presumably Hercules) would take on that task later.

After other adventures they eventually reached the land where the Golden Fleece was kept, Colchis. On Mount Olympus, Hera and Athena watched the young men and wondered how best to help them achieve their goal. The worst dangers were yet to come, and some help was sure to be needed.

Hera knew that if the Argonauts approached the palace and were seen by the guards, they would probably be killed. So she caused a dense fog to arise from the river, where the ship now sailed, and the Argonauts were able to get near the palace before anyone could spot them. But that was not enough. Together Athena and Hera went to Aphrodite and requested her help. Amazingly, she agreed and asked Eros to shoot one of his infallible arrows into the breast of Medea, the daughter of the king of Colchis, so that she would fall hopelessly in love with Jason and do everything she could to keep him safe.

The king received the visitors cautiously. He did not like strangers in his land. He asked Jason why he had come to his country, and Jason (who never would make a good politician) told the king immediately that he had come for the precious Golden Fleece, which, he insisted, belonged by rights to Greece.

Of course the king of Colchis was very angry. Here was a complete stranger, not just asking, but demanding his country's greatest treasure. But instead of having the Argonauts killed outright, he devised a trial, which, he was convinced, they could not pass and would result in their death.

With a false smile, he said to Jason, "The Fleece can belong only to the greatest hero in the universe. You will have to prove yourself to be such a hero, or, of course, I cannot give it to you. That would be an affront to Zeus. I therefore propose a trial of your courage and skill. If you pass it, I will let you have the Fleece without any further trouble."

The king owned two bulls whose feet were made of bronze, and whose breath was made of fire. They trampled anyone who came near them with their hooves or scalded the person to death with their breath. No one had ever been able to harness them to a plow. Jason would have to subdue the bulls and harness them to a plow, but that was not all. He would then have to take a sack of dragon's teeth and sow them in the plowed land, like seed corn. Instead of producing plants, the earth would bring forth a crop of armed men, also breathing fire. Jason would have to cut all of them down before he would be declared the winner and awarded the Golden Fleece.

Medea, in love with Jason, listened in horror to her father's suggestions. Fortunately for the moment (and unfortunately for the future, as it would turn out) Medea had been endowed at birth with powers of witchcraft. So she made up a magic ointment, which, when rubbed into someone's body, would keep that person safe from any harm. It is said that the plant from which the ointment was made contained drops of Prometheus's blood.

At night, when everyone in the palace was asleep, she met with Jason and gave him the ointment, carefully instructing him how to use it. Jason realized that Medea was in love with him, and, since she was a beautiful young woman, he thought that he loved her in return. He promised to take her back with him to Greece and to marry her as soon as he had obtained the Fleece.

Then Medea told him that when the armed, fire-breathing soldiers who grew from the dragon seed attacked him, he was to throw a stone in their midst, which would confuse them. They would turn against each other until all were killed.

Janus was delighted with the plan. He told Medea that all of Greece would forever be in her debt if he brought back the Golden Fleece, and that he would love her as long as he lived.

Medea, who, until Aphrodite caused her to fall so helplessly in love, had always given her first loyalty to her family, was heartbroken at her betrayal of her father. But she was powerless to fight against her feelings for Jason.

Jason did exactly what Medea had told him. He rubbed his body with her magic ointment, and the bulls could not touch him. He harnessed them and plowed the field. Then he sowed the dragon's teeth and an army of fire-breathing soldiers confronted him. He threw a stone in their midst, and just as Medea had predicted, they fought each other to the death. Jason won, and he went to the king to claim his prize.

However, the king had no intention of parting with the Fleece. He had not thought that Jason could pass the trial, but just in case the worst happened, he had kept one vital fact from Jason as a precaution. The Fleece was guarded by a terrible, huge serpent, which would attack and kill anyone who came near the treasure. Medea, however, knew about this monster and accompanied Jason when he went to get his prize. With magical incantations, she put the serpent to sleep so Jason could pick up the Fleece and go directly to the *Argo*, where his companions were waiting. As promised, he took Medea with him to return to Greece.

The king of Colchis was furious. He disowned and cursed his disloyal daughter. But he still had a son who might help him get back the Fleece. The son was ordered to follow Jason in a ship and to get the Fleece back. The chase was a long one, but eventually Medea saved Jason again, this time by an even more terrible deed, causing the death of her brother. She sent word to him that she wanted to return home and beg her father's forgiveness. She would meet him alone in a cave on an island. When her brother arrived, she was not alone. Jason was there with his sword drawn, and he killed the brother, who was unarmed and had suspected nothing. Without their leader the men the king had sent dispersed in confusion, and Jason and Medea went on to Greece.

When Jason arrived at home, he found that a terrible tragedy had occurred while he was away. Pelias had forced Jason's father to kill himself, and his mother had died of grief. Jason, who was no longer the innocent who had arrived several years before to reclaim his throne, now asked Medea to find a terrible revenge against Pelias. And Medea, who had once been a dutiful daughter and a loving sister, was so bewitched by her love for Jason that she would do anything he asked of her. So she befriended Pelias's daughters and told them she could use her power to turn their aging father into a gorgeous youth.

To prove what she could do, she cut up an old and stringy ram, put it in a pot of boiling water, and sprinkled the pot with her magic herbs. Out jumped a lamb—frisky, young, and healthy. Then she persuaded the king's daughters that she could perform a similar operation for their father. They gave him a powerful sleeping potion, and, while he was unconscious, at Medea's suggestion, they cut him up into pieces, just as she had the ram, and put the parts of his body into a kettle of boiling water. Of course, the king's daughters expected Medea to do her magic revival trick and bring their father out not only alive, but young. But Medea disappeared, and they were confronted with the body of their dead father. They were so appalled at what they had done that they committed suicide, and Jason was indeed revenged. But after such a deed, the pair could not remain in Iolcus.

Jason then took Medea to Corinth, where two sons were born to them. There they lived for ten years. But Jason was ambitious and not always heroic. When the playwright Euripides told the story of Jason's later years, it was the evil in his nature, rather than the heroism and beauty of his youth, that was most in evidence.

Jason wanted to be king of Corinth. One way to accomplish this was to marry the only daughter of the king of Corinth, so he asked for her hand in marriage. She was rich and beautiful, as well as in line to inherit the throne, and apparently Jason forgot entirely that he had sworn eternal fidelity to Medea, who had betrayed her family and her country for him.

He did not even bother to tell Medea of his forthcoming marriage. She heard about it when it was whispered among the women in the town square. At first she would not believe the story, but when preparations for the great wedding feast began, she could no longer ignore Jason's betrayal. In her anger, she made threats against Jason's new bride, and Jason, knowing that she was capable of magic, thought it best to remove her before she could do any harm. He asked the king of Corinth to have her and their two sons exiled.

Medea at first could not believe that the man for whom she had killed her brother would betray her and then send her and his own sons into exile, where they might have to live as slaves. She asked him to see her, and begged him to reconsider, but he told her coldly, "I could have had you killed when I heard that you were threatening my new bride, so be grateful that I am only sending you into exile. I am doing what is best for me and for this country by securing the succession to the throne. I will give you and our two sons an allowance to live on, but you must leave this place at once. I never want to see you again."

Medea protested that she had sacrificed her family, her country, and even her conscience for him. But her pleas were to no avail. Jason told her that she had saved him only because Aphrodite had forced her to love him, and that she had received sufficient reward from him by being taken from her uncivilized, uncultured country to Greece, the hub of the universe. He then gave her a bag of gold and ordered her to take herself and the children out of the country as quickly as possible.

Medea realized, for the first time, that she had been used. Probably Jason had never really loved her. He had kept her only as long as she suited his needs and ambitions. And her love for him turned to hatred. First she decided to get rid of the woman who was to become his new wife.

She knew that the princess was vain and loved beautiful clothing. So she spun and wove a dress of gold and silver that looked as if it had been fashioned from sun- and moonbeams. No one had ever seen as beautiful a garment as the one Medea made. Then she anointed the dress with a mysterious, invisible poison, and asked one of her sons to take it to the princess as a wedding present and peace offering. The princess was delighted with the lovely dress and tried it on immediately. But as soon as it touched her body, she felt as if she were engulfed in a fearful, searing fire. She could not take the garment off. It stuck to her and burned her to death. She died in terrible agony.

When Medea heard that the princess was dead, she knew that Jason would come to get his revenge. She also knew that, without her, her children were doomed to slavery at best, or to death at worst. In Euripides' words, she thought, "To die by other hands more merciless than mine; No, I who gave them life will give them death. . . ."

She stabbed both boys to death; and when Jason came, full of fury to take his vengeance on her, he found only the servants, mourning over the bodies of the two young children.

Medea had gone to the roof of her house, where a carriage, drawn by two dragons, was waiting for her. She flew away, followed by the curses of Jason. According to the Euripides story, Jason was heartbroken, but he blamed her, not himself, for what had happened.

Euripides, like most of the Greek playwrights of his time, portrayed neither Medea nor Jason as total villains. Medea betrayed her family because of her hopeless and helpless love for Jason, and killed her children not to revenge herself on her husband, but because she feared a future worse than death for them. Of course, the murder of her husband's future wife was motivated only by fury, jealousy, and revenge.

Jason betrayed Medea because of his love of power and probably because he was incapable of loving another human being selflessly. Perhaps, in his own way, he was also horrified at the many sins Medea had committed on his behalf and, realizing that she had acted to benefit him, wanted to get away from her. It must have occurred to him that the power she had to destroy could, conceivably, be turned against him some day. And, of course, it was.

Euripides does not make clear where Medea and her dragon coach went after they left Corinth, but in other stories she appears in Thebes and in Athens, and even, eventually, back in Colchis. It is said that when she died, she went to the Elysian Fields. Jason is said to have wandered homeless until, trying to relive past glories, he sat under the prow of the old, beached *Argo* and the prow fell and killed him.

Chapter 24

Oedipus: The Tragic Hero Who Might Have Asked "Why Me?"

SOURCES: The story of Oedipus is part of a long and tragic family saga, like several others in Greek mythology. The Oedipus myth probably was told and retold by various unknown poets and troubadors long before it came to fascinate one of Greece's greatest and most profound playwrights, Sophocles. Eventually he wrote not just one, but two plays about the tragic hero: *Oedipus the King* and *Oedipus at Colonus*. Both plays only allude to the family history and to the main events of Oedipus's life—the fact that he killed his father, Laius, and married his mother, Jocasta, thus fulfilling a prophecy made long before his birth. They concentrate only on the aftermath of these events. And how much of what Sophocles tells us belongs to old tradition and how much was new, we have no way of knowing.

What makes the Oedipus story different from most of the other Greek myths is that there seems to be no reason why so many terrible accidents happened, not only to him, but to his parents, grandparents, and other ancestors. There is some indication that Laius may have angered a god, but on the whole the members of the House of Thebes are generally described as noble, upstanding people. Those who were rulers were generally kind and brave. None seems to have been afflicted by hubris. Yet all of them were pursued by almost unimaginable misfortunes.

Some experts in Greek mythology have explained that the terrible fate that befell so many members of the Royal House of Thebes was to be seen as proof that suffering was not a punishment for sin or wrongdoing, and that the innocent as well as the guilty could be brought to great misery.

However, the late Eugene O'Neill, Jr., son of the American playwright Eugene O'Neill, and a great student of Greek drama, believed that calling the story of Oedipus "a tragedy of fate" is only partially true. He said, "Oedipus, in some sense, is presented as master of his own destiny, or else it is meaningless that at the end of the play he does not excuse himself by pleading that he did not know what he was doing, but rather accepts full responsibility as a moral agent of his acts, whether done in ignorance or not."

There is an indication in the second Sophocles play, *Oedipus at Colonus*—in which the king, of his own volition, decides the time has come for his death—that the gods and fate have forgiven him. At the end, Oedipus disappears mysteriously, without pain and suffering, and other characters agree that this is the best end for life.

The Oedipus tragedy has fascinated not only writers and moralists, but also those interested in psychology. One of the main tenents of psychiatry, as explained by Sigmund Freud, is the so-called Oedipus complex, which, according to that scholar, afflicts every male child: the envy and jealousy a boy feels toward his father for having married his mother. Other later psychologists have disputed this theory, but the idea remains.

THE STORY: King Laius of the royal House of Thebes married a distant cousin, Jocasta. Both were concerned about the royal succession and sent to the Oracle at Delphi to find out if they would have a son. The news that came back to them was terrible: A son would indeed be born to them, but he would kill his father and marry his mother.

King Laius, even though he should have known that Apollo's oracle always spoke the truth, tried to prevent the prophecy from happening. When a son was born to him and Jocasta, he had the baby's feet pierced and held together with a nail and left him on a lonely mountain path, expecting that he would die from the cold or be killed by wild beasts. Secure in the knowledge that his son would not be able to kill him, he and Jocasta continued to rule the kingdom.

For many years they lived in peace and security. Then King Laius decided to go on a journey. On the way home, he and all but one of his companions were killed by a stranger. The companion who returned safely to Thebes said they had been set upon by a robber.

The story was not as carefully investigated as it might have been, because at the time Thebes was under a terrible curse. A fierce monster, the Sphinx, threatened the whole city-state with starvation. No one could move in or out of the city because the Sphinx was always in the way. Shaped like a lion with wings, but with the face and the breasts of a woman, she would appear out of nowhere, and put a riddle to anyone she saw on the road. If the puzzle was not solved correctly, the wayfarer would be killed and eaten. No one could guess the answer to the riddle, and consequently no food supplies came to those who lived in the city. The people ate all their livestock, and finally even the rats and mice. But the Sphinx continued to lie in wait outside the gates, and the famine in the city grew worse and worse.

The sad story of the Thebans had reached neighboring islands and cities and occasionally, an especially brave young hero would attempt to find the Sphinx and answer the question. But none succeeded.

One day from nearby Corinth, a handsome and brilliant young prince called Oedipus made the journey to Thebes. He was thought to be the son of the king of Corinth, Polybus, and he had been told that the Delphic Oracle had predicted that he would kill his father. So he generally stayed as far away from Corinth as possible, especially when his father was in residence. When he heard about the plight of the Thebans, he resolved to help them. After all, his life was not worth much to him. If the Sphinx killed him, at least his father, Polybus, would be safe.

So he walked right up to the Sphinx and asked to be given the riddle. "What creature goes on four feet in the morning, two at noon, and three in the evening?" the monster asked. Oedipus, unlike all the others who had tried to solve the puzzle, knew the answer right away.

"Human beings," he said. "As infants they creep on hands and feet; as adults they walk upright on two feet; and in old age they use their feet, plus a stick to keep from falling." The Sphinx was so ashamed of having been outsmarted that she killed herself. In some stories, Oedipus kills her with his sword.

The Thebans were so grateful to the young hero that they offered him the crown of the kingdom and the hand of Jocasta, their queen, in marriage. For many years they ruled happily together, and had four children—two sons and two daughters.

But suddenly, when the children of Oedipus and Jocasta had grown into adulthood, everything changed. Thebes was visited by a series of terrible plagues. Harvests failed, herds died. Diseases that no one could cure or prevent hit the population. Seeing his people suffer was terrible for Oedipus. He felt that in some way, for some reason, the gods must be angry and be punishing those who lived in the country. So he sent his wife's brother, Creon, to

Delphi to ask the Oracle what had gone wrong, and whether there was anything he could do to free his people from what seemed to be a terrible curse.

Creon returned with surprising news. Apollo, through the Oracle, had said that all the misfortunes would be lifted from the people of Corinth if the person who had killed King Laius was punished.

Oedipus was glad that there finally was something he could do to relieve the misery of his people. He let it be known that anyone who had any information about the long ago crime should come forward. Nobody did. Then he remembered that in Thebes there was an ancient blind prophet who had solutions to puzzles that no one else could solve. He sent for the prophet. But much to his surprise, the old man refused to answer any questions. "Those who seek the source of certain mysteries will suffer terrible tortures," he said.

But Oedipus remained adamant. Eventually he even accused the old prophet of being the murderer himself. Otherwise, why would he not tell what he knew?

Finally the prophet had to speak to avoid being executed for a crime he had not committed. "You, yourself, are the murderer," he told Oedipus.

Oedipus at first became exceedingly angry, but then decided that the prophet had become senile and was, therefore, no longer reliable. He sent him home.

He continued to talk over the strange mystery with his wife, Jocasta, and she agreed that the prophet had, of course, been wrong. She told him that the Oracle at Delphi had told them, many years before, that King Laius would be murdered by their son, and that they had made very sure that this could not happen by having the baby killed soon after its birth.

"So you see, you can't trust prophets or oracles, no matter what the priests tell you," she said. "My first husband was murdered by robbers where the three roads meet on the way to Delphi."

"When did this murder happen?" Oedipus asked.

"Oh, six or eight months before you came to Thebes," Jocasta said.

"How many men were with the king when he was killed?"

asked Oedipus.

"Five altogether," Jocasta answered. "Four were killed, and only one survived. He came to the palace as soon as he could and told us what had happened."

"You must send for this messenger at once," Oedipus ordered.

When the messenger entered the throne room, his face went white with horror. "There is the man who killed the old king," he said, pointing at Oedipus. And Oedipus remembered an incident he had forgotten. On his way to Thebes, he had come on a party of five men. Apparently, the travelers considered him to be a robber. They attacked him, and in self-defense he had killed four of them. One ran away.

"It is possible that I killed Laius, but why is Apollo so angry?" asked Oedipus. "I was being attacked. If I had not killed him and his companions, they would have killed me."

"And besides," said Jocasta, "the Oracle of Apollo was wrong. It told us that the king would be killed by his son. You are certainly not his son. You are the son of King Polybus of Corinth."

But then a series of coincidences occurred that no one had expected, and soon everyone's assumptions about what had happened in the past were destroyed.

A messenger arrived, announcing the death of King Polybus from natural causes. At first Oedipus was vastly relieved. After all, the oracle had told him that he would kill his father, whom he assumed to be Polybus, and the king was now dead. The messenger, however, had some additional news. "You are not the son of King Polybus," he told Oedipus. "He adopted you when you were a tiny baby. As a matter of fact, I brought you to him myself. You were given to me by a shepherd, who found you on a mountain path near Thebes. He thought that you had been left there to die. It was said that King Laius had ordered his firstborn son to be exposed to certain death because of a prophecy. And all of us thought that you might be that unfortunate child."

Oedipus, still not understanding what was happening, asked the messenger to find the old shepherd who had rescued him. The shepherd confirmed the story and added that the infant's feet had been pierced by a nail.

When Queen Jocasta heard this last detail, she turned chalky-white, and ran from the room. And finally Oedipus himself understood. He had thought himself safe from the terrible prophecy of Apollo. But the prophecy had not lied. He had indeed murdered his real father, King Laius, and married his mother, Jocasta.

He cried out in agony. "I am accursed and so are all my children. No wonder the people of Thebes are being punished with famine and plague. I am the murderer to whom Apollo is pointing. There is no help for any of us. We must all die."

He rushed to his chamber to find his wife, who was also his mother. But he was too late. The terrible truth had been too much for her. She had hanged herself with her scarf, and was dead.

Oedipus first thought of killing himself, too, but he considered this insufficient punishment for the terrible sin that had been committed. Instead, he used his dagger to put out his eyes. He felt he was no longer worthy of looking at the bright world in which he had lived so happily. From now on, he would live in darkness.

Oedipus, of course, resigned the throne. His two sons, who were now considered illegitimate, were no longer in the line of succession. Jocasta's brother, Creon, became the regent of the country. But still the plagues did not lift. Finally Creon, on the advice of prophets, sent Oedipus into exile. His daughter, Antigone, insisted on accompanying him. But no country wanted to accept a man who had killed his own father and married his mother.

Finally, Theseus of Athens (see Chapter 22), who was one of the kindest and most compassionate men of his time, invited the unfortunate blind man and his daughter to come to his court, where he attempted to comfort him. Theseus pointed out that nothing that had happened had really been his fault. It had all been the will of the gods, which no one could understand, and that his fate had been determined even before his birth. But Oedipus could not forgive himself.

Theseus suggested that Oedipus go to Colonus, a lovely spot near Athens, where there was a place that was sacred to those who felt insupportable guilt and needed forgiveness from the gods. Oedipus followed the suggestion, and eventually at Colonus he heard the same voice of the Oracle that had prophesied such a terrible future for him, tell him that he was now forgiven. Oedipus died alone at Colonus, and his body vanished mysteriously. Many thought that the gods had taken him away, perhaps to the Elysian Fields or some other, happier place to atone for the misery they had caused him while he was alive.

Chapter 25

Antigone: A Hero Can Also Be a Woman

SOURCES: In Greek mythology, there are almost no women who are either physically or morally heroic. In fact, Antigone is, perhaps, the only female who possesses all the qualities Greeks most admired in men: physical courage, loyalty, and the determination to do right, even at the cost of her own life.

Antigone appears as a minor character in many of the tales about Oedipus. But she is one of the most important characters in the play *Antigone,* by Sophocles, which tells of the final, tragic end of the whole House of Thebes. In this play, as in all of his work, Sophocles makes few judgments. Although in most other versions of the story the character of Creon, who orders Antigone killed because she refuses to obey what she considers an immoral order, appears as an unmitigated villain, Sophocles sees him as a tortured man who feels that the laws of the state must be obeyed.

Although he depicts Antigone as a true heroine for her insistence on doing what she considers right, he also sees another quality in her: a kind of fanaticism, displayed by many of those who insist that they must follow their own conscience against all odds. In Sophocles' view, Antigone, who was incapable of compromise, was in a way responsible for her own death. What Sophocles valued most was moderation, a quality he found lacking in both the dictator and the martyred heroine. Therefore, both in their own way had committed sins against the gods, although, of course, Creon's sin was the most serious.

THE STORY: Even after the deaths of Laius, Jocasta, and Oedipus, the tragedy that would eventually wipe out the entire Royal House of Thebes continued.

Creon had been made regent by Oedipus, who had decided that neither of his two sons could legitimately rule the city, since, under the laws of the state and the gods, they were both the product of an unnatural union. But the sons, Polynices and Eteocles, did not agree. Each felt that he was the rightful ruler of Thebes, not his mother's brother Creon, whom Oedipus had named. Each wanted to be the sole ruler. Eteocles succeeded in staging a palace revolution and overthrew Creon. He then expelled his brother from Thebes. Polynices took refuge on a nearby island and did all he could to arouse the enmity of other neighboring states against Thebes. Then he collected an army to attack the city.

All this time Antigone was at the court of Theseus. And her sister, Ismene, had joined her there when she heard that their father was dying. Both decided to go home to Thebes after his death, and were given an escort by Theseus to see them safely on their way. When they arrived, they found the city in an uproar: One brother, with a group of allies, was marching against the city, and the other was determined to hold it at all costs. Meanwhile, Creon had not given up his own ambition to rule Thebes. His course was simply to wait for the two brothers to destroy each other and leave the city without a legitimate ruler. Then he would take over again.

Thebes was besieged by an army led by one son of Oedipus, and defended by an army led by the other son. Under siege, the population of the city was starving. But the invading army also was gaining no advantage, and disease and hunger were depleting its warriors as well.

Finally, both sides decided that the war should be settled by hand-to-hand combat between the two brothers. If Eteocles was the winner, the invading army led by Polynices would withdraw and Eteocles would become king. On the other hand, if Polynices won, Eteocles would give up, go into exile, and his brother would be the ruler.

As it turned out, neither won. They killed each other in the battle. As he lay dying, Polynices begged to be buried in his homeland.

With both brothers dead, Creon was back in control. He decided that Eteocles, who had defended the city against an invading army (even though he had overthrown his uncle), should be buried with every honor due a dead king. However, Polynices, the invader, should be left unburied outside of the city, where vultures and wild dogs would devour his body.

According to Greek law and religion, this was a vengeance of which the gods did not approve. The souls of the unburied could not fly across the river Styx to the land of the dead, but were condemned to wander forever in desolation, with no resting place anywhere in the universe. To bury the dead was considered a sacred duty. Anyone who came upon a dead body was obliged to arrange a burial, even if the dead person were a total stranger.

Creon, in his proclamation, changed this holy law. Not only did he prohibit anyone from burying his nephew, he ordered that anyone who tried to do so should be put to death.

Antigone and Ismene heard with horror what Creon had ordered. Ismene suggested that her sister sprinkle earth on their brother's body. According to religious law, this gesture might count as a legitimate burial. But Antigone's high principles would not allow her to take the easy way out. When a thick dust storm arose, she left the city without being seen, found her brother's dead body, and buried him.

Some hours later, the guards Creon had placed around the body realized what had happened. When Creon threatened to punish the guards, Antigone stepped forward and told him what she had done.

"You knew of my proclamation?" he asked her. Many of the

bystanders felt that he was hoping Antigone would deny ever having heard of the order. In that case he might be able to find her innocent of deliberate disobedience and forgive her. But Antigone would not lie.

"I knew of your law," she said. "But your edict transgresses that of the gods. The unwritten laws of heaven are not of today nor yesterday, but for all time."

Ismene, finally finding her own courage, insisted that she had helped her sister, but Antigone would not let her take any of the blame. "She did nothing to help me," she said. And she told her sister not to take any of the responsibility. "The truth is that your choice was to live, and mine to die," she told her.

As she was led away, she spoke to the bystanders: "Behold me, what I suffer because I have upheld that which is high."

There are no stories about what became of Ismene. She simply disappeared. It is assumed that she went into exile and never married or had children, and that, with the death of Antigone, the royal family of Thebes was wiped out. Doubly so, because in some accounts one son of Creon died in the battle, and the other, engaged to Antigone, chose to die with her.

PART FIVE

Popular Legends and Fairy Tales

Chapter 26

Orpheus and Eurydice

SOURCES: Like many other early Greek love stories, the origin of this tale is lost in the past. The best written versions come to us from the Roman poets Ovid and Virgil. However, the third-century B.C. Greek writer Apollonius of Rhodes mentions the character of Orpheus in his story of the Argonauts. It is obvious that he expected his readers to know who Orpheus was, although he does not tell us anything about Eurydice. Also, pictures of a man and a woman that some experts have identified as possibly being the two lovers appear on some very early Greek pottery.

The story has fascinated writers and artists through the centuries. There are many paintings, plays, operas, and ballets about the lovers, some created very recently. Occasionally, an artist wishes to give the sad tale a happy ending. In an opera about Orpheus and Eurydice, the eighteenth-century German composer Christoph Gluck hints that they both were allowed to go to the Elysian Fields, where they could live happily ever after. This idea was picked up by twentieth-century choreographer George Balanchine, who, in his ballet *Chaconne*, also has the couple dancing happily in the Elysian Fields. However, in another ballet, *Orpheus*, he sticks closely to the best-known version. Eurydice is sent back to the underworld, and Orpheus is torn apart by demons.

THE STORY: Orpheus was the son of a muse, and considered by all who heard him to be the greatest musician in the world. He played a small, stringed instrument called a lyre, the instrument played by Apollo himself.

When Orpheus played and sang, he had power over everyone and everything that heard him: not only all humans, but animals, flowers, and even rocks and water.

He met and married a young woman, Eurydice, with whom he was desperately in love. But their joy was short-lived. As Eurydice walked into a meadow with her bridesmaids, she was stung by a viper and died. Some of his friends said that the gods were jealous of the couple's happiness and would not allow a mortal man and woman to live in such bliss.

Orpheus was inconsolable. He decided that he could not live without Eurydice, so he would dare what no mortal man had ever dared before: He would follow her into Hades and beg the dark powers to give her back to him. He undertook the terrible journey into the underworld, charming with his beautiful music all the monsters and other mythical creatures who tried to stop him. Even the dog, Cerberus, who was supposed to guard the gates of the underworld, stood motionless and stopped his snarling as Orpheus, playing his lyre, passed by. The faces of the terrible Furies, charged with keeping those who belonged in the world of the dead from trying to escape, were wet with tears at the wonderful sounds that Orpheus's lyre made, and let him pass.

Even Hades could not resist the powerful appeal of the young man's music. He summoned Eurydice and gave her back to her husband, with one condition. She would have to follow him out of the underworld, keeping several paces behind him. He would not be allowed to look back at her until they were both back in the sunlight.

As Orpheus walked out of Hades, he could hear his wife's footsteps behind him, and he longed to see her and to make sure that she was really following him back to earth. But he controlled himself until he had stepped through the opening of the cave that was the entrance to the underworld. Then he looked back, holding out his arms to embrace his beloved wife. But he was too early. Eurydice had not yet walked into the light. The instant he saw her, she slipped back into the darkness, never to return.

Orpheus desperately tried to follow her, but this time he was not allowed to go. In some versions of the story, his shock had made it impossible for him to play his instrument. In other versions, a Fury or some other mysterious monster snatched the instrument from his hands. At any rate, the power to charm away the dark creatures failed him.

So he was forced to stop at the gate of the underworld, and eventually to return back to earth. In some versions of the story, he continued to play his lyre, but his songs were so sad that no one wanted to listen to them. In other versions, he could not find his lyre, and just wandered the earth, desolate and alone. Eventually he was discovered by a band of Maenads—the mad followers of the god of wine, Dionysus—who tore him limb from limb and flung his head into a swift river. The river bore the disembodied head to an island, where the Muses found it and buried it.

The inhabitants of several islands claim to own Orpheus's final resting place, and all of them tell visitors that the birds there sing more sweetly than anywhere else on earth to honor the greatest musician the world has ever known: Orpheus, who loved his wife so much that he followed her to the land of death, and was unable to bring her back, even for only a second.

Chapter 27 *Midas*

SOURCES: The legend of Midas is, unlike almost all Greek myths, a morality tale. It is best told by Ovid, a Roman poet, but many of the themes in the story appear in other ancient folklore. Experts believe that Ovid got at least the outline of the plot from a Greek poem or tale he heard or read, but that was somehow lost to literature.

THE STORY: Midas was the king of Phrygia, known as the land of the roses, and he had a great rose garden surrounding his palace. One day a follower of the wine god, Dionysus, strayed into that garden and fell drunk into one of the flower beds.

Midas's servants made fun of the man, bound him up with garlands of roses, and took him, as a joke, to the king. Midas, however, recognized that there was something special about this guest and entertained him royally for ten days. Then Dionysus appeared to reclaim his friend, and, because Midas had shown true hospitality, asked him to make one wish. Whatever he wished for would happen.

Midas was already a rich man, but he had always wanted to be the richest in the world. So he made a very stupid request: He asked that whatever he touched should turn into gold. Of course, Dionysus knew when he granted this favor that Midas would have to come back to ask it to be revoked. But Midas did not know this until he tried to put food and water into his mouth and they turned into metal. No matter how precious gold is, it cannot sustain life.

So the king hurried back to the god and implored him to revoke the fatal gift. Dionysus obliged. He told Midas to go and wash at the source of the river Pactolus, and he would be able to eat and drink like a normal person again. Midas obeyed the god's suggestion, and many tourists in Greece today are told that somewhere in that country there is a river in which remains of Midas's gold can be found. All one has to do is search for it.

But more misfortune awaited poor Midas. He was asked to serve as a judge in a musical contest between Pan and Apollo. Pan was only a minor god who played amusing tunes on his flute made of reeds. Apollo, on the other hand, played heavenly music on his silver lyre. Besides, he was a much more powerful god than Pan. The other judge, a minor mountain god called Tmolus, gave the prize to Apollo. Midas, who was apparently not a classical music lover, and who, besides, did not recognize superior power when confronted with it, awarded the prize to Pan.

Apollo, of course, was very angry. Because he considered Midas to have no sense about music, he gave him the ears of a donkey. This was a very embarrassing thing to happen to a king. So, in order to keep his deformity from his family and his subjects, Midas had a cap made that carefully hid his donkey ears. Only the barber who cut his hair knew the secret, and he had to swear a solemn oath never to reveal it to anybody.

Secrets are hard to keep, especially when they concern one's king, but the barber tried hard not to gossip about Midas's misfortune. But one day, he simply could not contain himself any longer. So he dug a deep hole in a field and whispered into it: "Midas has donkey ears." Then he filled the hole up with earth, thinking that the secret was still safe.

Apollo, however, was not yet finished with Midas. He saw to it that weeds grew over the hole, and when they were stirred by the wind, they whispered: "King Midas has donkey ears." Soon everyone knew the truth, and even condemning the unfortunate barber to death did not keep the king's subjects from laughing.

The story actually has two morals. The first one—that excessive greed can lead to disaster—would probably be accepted by most of us today. The second—that in a dispute between a strong and a weak contestant it is safest to side with the strong one—is cynical at best. But the Greeks (and Ovid) were realists, and probably considered this a lesson worth learning.

Chapter 28 *Pygmalion*

SOURCES: There have been myths and fairy tales about statues or dolls turning into living human beings in many cultures. One of the best known is Pygmalion, which is probably a Greek fable that was told by storytellers in many places and at various times. However, the only written version we know is by the Roman poet Ovid.

The British dramatist George Bernard Shaw interpreted the Pygmalion theme in his own way. In his story, a gentleman who is also an expert in elegant speech makes a bet with a friend that he can turn a Cockney flower girl—who speaks English with a terrible accent, does not wash, and has no manners—into a duchess within a matter of weeks. He will teach her proper English, good taste, and cleanliness. He wins his bet: Within a few months he passes off Eliza the flower seller as Eliza the duchess. This story was the basis of one of the most successful musicals of all times, *My Fair Lady*.

The idea of changing something or someone into an ideal being is obviously of interest to many artists. The Greek story of Pygmalion is a perfect example of such a fable.

THE STORY: On the island of Cyprus there lived a gifted young sculptor named Pygmalion. Some say he was just a sculptor, and some say he was also king of Cyprus. He was very handsome, and many of the local maidens tried to make him fall in love with them. But he let it be known that he was not interested in love or marriage: His art was all he needed to be happy. Besides, he told anyone who cared to listen, he could sculpt a more beautiful and perfect woman out of marble than any he had seen made out of flesh and blood.

His favorite project was the statue of a young woman, on which he worked for a long time. Every day he would make small changes, and add extra touches to make her ever more beautiful and graceful. And all those who saw his work of art had to admit that she was lovelier than any human woman had ever been.

One day Pygmalion went to his studio to make yet another small change on his masterpiece, but, he realized, there was nothing left to change. She was absolutely perfect as she was. And what's more, he had fallen hopelessly in love with her.

The young women he had rejected now laughed at him. They had their revenge. The sculptor, who had ignored them, was now appropriately punished. He had found the one woman he could love; but, unfortunately, since she was made of marble and ivory, she would never be able to return his feelings. And Pygmalion became more unhappy with every day that passed. He loved a lifeless statue, which could never return his affection.

Cyprus was the island where, according to legend, Aphrodite had risen from the ocean foam. So every year people organized a huge festival to her. They decorated her temples and made sacrifices of the most beautiful flowers and the best tasting fruit to their patron goddess. They danced and sang and gave parties in her honor.

During one festival, Aphrodite noticed the sad young man who was unable to rejoice in human love. She decided that, since he had been so faithful to a lifeless statue, he deserved her help. (One of the few times, incidentally, that Aphrodite made up her mind to do something unselfish and kind.)

She appeared before Pygmalion and asked him what she could do for him. He begged that she create, somewhere, a woman as perfect as his statue.

"Actually, you have already created the perfect woman," the goddess said. "I will simply breathe life into her . . . and you will have exactly what you want."

Suddenly Pygmalion saw a flame leap up at the base of his masterpiece. Still doubting that the Goddess of Love had really performed a miracle for him, he carefully touched the statue's hand. It was warm and soft. He embraced her. Her entire body had turned from stone into flesh. He kissed her, and she kissed him back.

Hand in hand with his now-living creation, he ran down to the festival. Others at first refused to believe what they saw. They thought a new young woman who happened to look exactly like the statue had moved to the island. To avoid any misunderstandings, Aphrodite appeared and assured everyone that she had turned the statue into a woman. Her name would, from now on, be Galatea. So Galatea and Pygmalion got married. And, unlike what usually happens in Greek myths, they lived happily ever after.

Chapter 29

Narcissus and Other Flowers

SOURCES: Much of Greece is barren and rocky, but in the spring the hillsides come alive with beautiful flowers in many colors. Gathering wild flowers is a favorite pastime among those who live in or visit the Greek countryside, and probably the early Greeks, who first told the myths, enjoyed the same activity.

Like many other civilizations, the Greeks believed the gods were the source of their lovely spring flowers. Since they admired humans sufficiently to cast their gods in human form, it seems natural that they thought the most beautiful blossoms might once have been human beings.

Many of the flower myths go back to the earliest folktales. Some are repeated in Homeric legends, but the best retellings available to us come from the Romans.

NARCISSUS AND ECHO

THE STORY: Narcissus was such a handsome young man that everyone who saw him fell in love with him. But he was not interested in love. No young woman was good enough for him. Wherever he went, women tried to tempt him, but he just told them to go away.

Nymphs also fell in love with the gorgeous Narcissus. Among them was a lovely nymph called Echo. Hera, on an expedition to discover which of the nymphs was Zeus's latest love, was diverted by Echo's chatter until all the nymphs had fled. As a result, Hera, annoyed with Echo and herself, decreed that, "From now on you will not be able to say one word on your own. You will only be able to repeat the last few words of what another person has said."

Now Echo was at an even greater disadvantage in trying to pursue Narcissus. The young man had paid no attention to her before, when she called to him. Now she could only sadly repeat his words when he talked to her. "Go away," he would say. "Away," poor Echo would moan. "Leave me alone," Narcissus would cry. "Alone," Echo would repeat.

Eventually Echo became so saddened and embarrassed by her situation that she hid in mountain groves and caves, where, even today, she still answers travelers' calls by repeating their last words.

Meanwhile, Narcissus had finally found someone he could love. He had looked into a pool of clear water and seen his own face gazing back at him: the most beautiful face he had ever observed. When he realized that he could love no one but himself, he pined away and died of a broken heart. (According to another version of the legend, he became so fascinated with his image in the lake that he leaned over too far, fell in, and drowned. And in still another version, he killed himself with a dagger.)

The nymphs whom he had scorned were so saddened by his death that they sought his body and buried him near the pool where he had seen his own face. On his grave a beautiful flower appeared. It was named after him: the narcissus. Incidentally, as described by the Greek and Roman poets, the narcissus was not the white and yellow flower we know, but a beautiful *purple* blossom, like an iris.

HYACINTH

Hyacinth was an exceedingly handsome young man, whom Apollo loved and admired. He often took him along as his companion when he made his journeys to earth. Sometimes they competed at their favorite sport, discus throwing.

One day Apollo accidentally threw his discus so that it hit Hyacinth in the forehead. Horror-struck, the god tried to save his friend, but it was too late. Blood was gushing from Hyacinth's forehead, and, within a few minutes, he was dead. But all around him the bloodstained grass turned into a garden of beautiful purple flowers, which, from then on, became known as hyacinths.

According to another version of the story, the north wind, who also loved Apollo, was jealous of the god's affection for the human Hyacinth, and blew the discus directly at his head. At any rate, the result was the same: The young man died, and a flower was born.

ADONIS

Adonis was another beautiful young man whose untimely death brought about the creation of a flower. (In Greek myths, women, no matter how beautiful, generally don't turn into flowers, even if they die young and by accident.)

When Adonis was a baby, Aphrodite seized him and took him down to Hades for Persephone to guard. This was a serious mistake. Adonis grew to be so beautiful that even in the darkness of the underworld Persephone could see enough to fall in love with him. And, of course, Aphrodite, herself, loved him. So Aphrodite and Persephone went to Zeus to get him to decide who would be in charge of the handsome Adonis. Zeus did not want to cause any trouble, so he made what he considered a fair arrangement: Adonis would spend six months with each of the two—autumn and winter with Persephone, and summer and spring with Aphrodite.

Adonis loved to hunt, and, although hunting was not usually one of her favorite occupations, Aphrodite accompanied him when he went out to shoot wild animals. One fine spring day Adonis went hunting for boar, the wild pig that when irritated can become exceedingly dangerous. Adonis shot an arrow at a boar, but only wounded him. The boar turned on the young man and killed him with his big tusks.

Aphrodite was heartbroken. She tried to heal his wound, but he had already lost so much blood that he died. And on the spot of earth where he lay, a beautiful, blood-red flower grew. It was, incidentally, *not* called "the adonis," but "the anemone," although no one knows why. And its crimson flowers appear on Greek hillsides every spring to remind everyone of the beautiful young man who was loved by both Aphrodite and Persephone.

For more than two thousand years the Greek god Apollo has symbolized the arts: drama, poetry, music, painting, and sculpture. Here he is in person, in the twentieth-century ballet *Apollo*, by George Balanchine. The performers are (from left to right) *Maria Calegari, Peter Martins, Suzanne Farrell,* and *Kyra Nichols.*

The Temple of Tholos at Delphi.

From one of the temples at Delphi, one can see fields and mountains in the far distance. At dawn and at twilight, the place looks as mysterious today as it must have thousands of years ago, when troubled people came to that temple to seek help from the oracle to solve their problems.

Zeus used to turn himself into various species of animals when he was wooing beautiful but shy young women. One of his favorite transformations was into a swan.

Oak trees can live for a long time—indeed, ancient Greeks may have believed that they lived forever. This may be the reason the oak was the tree dedicated to Zeus and why many ancient oak trees can be seen in towns and villages all over Greece.

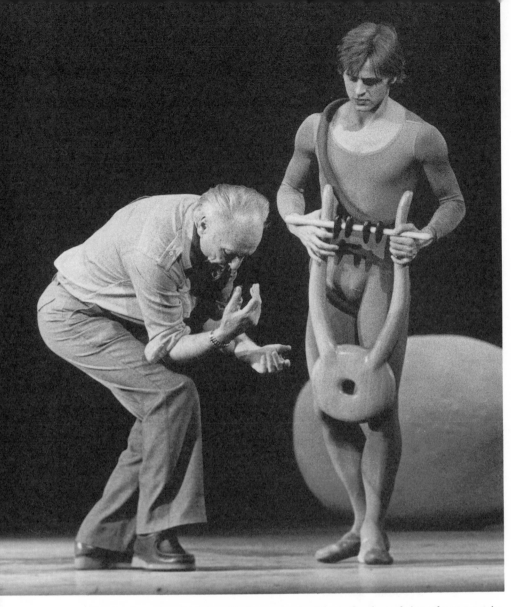

The tragic poet and singer, Orpheus, survived from Greek myth into the present in drama, opera, theater, and dance. Here is ballet star Mikhail Baryshnikov learning the principal role in Orpheus from choreographer George Balanchine.

The Odeon Theater, at the foot of the Acropolis. Probably much of the most famous music was performed there. Similar theaters have survived the centuries in many parts of Greece, and some of them are still used for outdoor theater today.

Light and fire gave man joy and wisdom. So the hero Prometheus (who gave man fire against Zeus's orders and who paid dearly for his courage) carries his flame to the twentieth century in Rockefeller Center, New York City, with the lights of the Christmas tree gleaming behind him and the skaters in the plaza enjoying the spectacle.

The entrance to the deadly maze at Knossos.

Statues of figures from Greek mythology can be seen in parks, squares, and museums for today's art lovers to enjoy. There are many such statues in the Piazza della Signoria in Florence, Italy. Among them is a beautiful but rather gruesome statue of Perseus holding the severed head of the Medusa.

*A statue of the god Dionysus
in Florence, Italy.*

This is the cave in which, local people tell us, Odysseus hid from his enemies during his first days home after the Trojan War, though the Odyssey itself says he stayed in a hut.

When Zeus was an infant he was nursed with milk from a mountain goat. She may have looked very much like this one, who is roaming a Greek hillside today.

As long as anyone's great-grandfather can remember, a pelican has stood waiting to look over any visitors about to take the boat to the island of Delos, where Apollo is said to have been born. Who knows—perhaps he was there on Apollo's birthday.

Many of the shores of mainland Greece and the Greek islands are rocky and treacherous. It is on a shore much like this one that ships coming home from the Trojan War might have been wrecked.

Hades abducting Persephone. The statue is in the Villa Borghese in Rome.

PART SIX

The Trojan War

Chapter 30

The Greeks and the Trojans

SOURCES: Most people believe that the entire story of the Trojan War comes to us from Homer's *Iliad*. That is not true. The *Iliad* starts when nine-tenths of the tale has already happened. The Greeks have been laying siege to Troy for nine years; the *Iliad* tells us of the events that take up, perhaps, fifty days, and ends with the death and burial of the Trojan Hector. This occurs some time before the final defeat of Trojan armies and the sack of the city. The *Iliad* does not include any of the aftermaths of the Greek victory, including the wanderings of Odysseus or the tragedy of Agamemnon and his family (see Chapter 32).

Many of the incidents that are part of the Trojan War legend come to us from the Greek playwrights, who must have used earlier sources, either written or oral, as a basis for their dramas.

The beauty contest between the three goddesses and the judgment made by the Trojan prince Paris are described in a play by Euripides. One version of the sacrifice of Iphigenia, the daughter of Agamemnon, which allowed the Greek ships to sail toward Troy after months of stormy seas, also is found in a drama by Euripides. The end of the Trojan War is fully described in the work of the Roman poet Virgil, and, in a completely different spirit, in one of the greatest antiwar plays of all time, *The Trojan Women*, by Euripides.

The story of the Trojan War is complicated and has dozens of characters, each of whom might well be the hero of an entirely separate story. So, the entire epic actually weaves together what many different writers have told of the events that occurred among both the Trojans and the Greeks. Frequently there are divergent points of view. For instance, Virgil, who considered war and battle as glorious shows of patriotism, gives us a triumphant victory poem, while Euripides, who was horrified by bloodshed and cruelty, gives us a powerful pacifist message.

Other plays and legends tell us what happened to many of the main characters after Troy was destroyed and the various Greek leaders went home. It is interesting to note that not one of the main characters comes to a happy and peaceful end, except Odysseus, whose adventures after he leaves Troy are also told to us by Homer (see Chapter 32).

Many scholars have speculated as to whether or not there was a real Troy, and whether the heroes and villains on both sides of the Trojan walls were people who actually lived more than twelve hundred years before Christ.

Archaeologists have long tried to find evidence of a historical Troy. Many believe that the ruins of a city on the Aegean coast of Turkey may have been Troy. But these ruins were found in layers: One city was obviously built on top of another, as various cities were destroyed either by war or natural disaster. However, it does seem as if somewhere in the middle of those layers there is indeed a place that matches several of Homer's descriptions.

There is, of course, little evidence that there were real people like Troy's King Priam, his sons Paris and Hector, the Greek King Agamemnon, the beautiful Helen (who caused all the trouble), and the many other heroes and heroines. There is evidence that the ancient fortress that may have been Troy was attacked at least once by an invading army, and probably burned. However, in the century in which the Trojan War would most probably have taken place, armies of pirate ships roamed the Aegean Sea, and these professional sackers of cities would not require the excuse of a beautiful kidnapped queen to attack a likely target. The chances are that whatever war occurred in the area Homer described was caused by greed, the desire to annex territory, or commercial competition between various rulers—the same elements that have always caused wars.

THE STORY: The gods on Olympus were having a party: the wedding of King Peleus to the sea nymph Thetis. All the gods and goddesses had been invited except Eris, the goddess of discord, whom, understandably enough, nobody liked, and who rarely was asked to any important Olympian events.

Furious at having been left out again, she decided to make trouble. She threw a golden apple marked "For the Fairest" into the banquet hall. Of course, all the goddesses wanted to claim it; but the choice narrowed down to three of the most powerful and most beautiful among them: Aphrodite, Hera, and Athena. Zeus was asked to judge to whom the apple should go, but he wisely refused to make such a choice. The goddesses insisted that he at least suggest a proper judge, and, to get himself out of the bind, he suggested a young man who, he assured everyone, was a superb judge of beauty.

Near Mount Ida, he said, was a young prince called Paris. He was the son of King Priam of Troy, but had been ordered to leave the city because of a prophecy that someday he would bring misfortune to his country and everyone who lived in it. At the moment he was working as a shepherd.

Paris, although almost as handsome as any god, was neither intelligent nor tactful. If he had had any sense or wisdom, he would have refused to undertake the task put to him by the three goddesses who appeared in the meadow where he was guarding his sheep. The goddesses were so eager to win the apple that they would not even allow themselves to be judged on their own merits. Each offered Paris a bribe.

Hera promised that if he chose her she would make him the lord of Europe and Asia. Athena said that she would make him a great warrior, who would lead the Trojans against their traditional enemies, the Greeks. The Trojans would win an overwhelming victory, leaving Greece in ruins. (Why Athena, who was the patron of Athens, would make such a promise is never clear.) Aphrodite promised him the most beautiful woman in the world for his wife.

Paris, besides being undiplomatic and not too bright, was more interested in women than he was in ruling a country, so he chose Aphrodite, and gave her the apple. Naturally, Hera and Athena were furious. They swore eternal enmity not only toward the young prince, but to his family and his country.

The most beautiful woman in the world turned out to be Helen, who, unfortunately, was married already. When she was still a young girl, the reports of her beauty had circulated throughout the world, and every young prince who heard of her wanted to marry her.

Many of these princes came from powerful families, and Helen's stepfather (her real father was supposed to be Zeus himself) feared that if he selected one man among the suitors, the others would all unite against him. He would then become involved in a war he could only lose. So he made all the suitors promise that they would uphold the honor of any man who might be picked to marry the lovely girl. Each of the princes, thinking that he would be the chosen one, made a solemn oath to champion the cause of Helen's husband against all enemies.

The stepfather chose Menelaus, the brother of Agamemnon. He was king of Sparta, which made him a very good match. However, he was also considerably older than his bride, and, by all accounts, neither attractive nor interesting. The marriage was not a successful one, but Helen retained her reputation as the most beautiful woman in the world. She was the woman Aphrodite had in mind for Paris, when she made her offer. Aphrodite herself had never taken marriage very seriously, and the fact that Helen already had a husband did not seem to bother her. She led Paris straight to Sparta, where, as the son of a king from another country, he was received as an honored guest. Under the rules of Greek hospitality, the bonds between a guest and host were sacred. Neither was supposed to do the other any harm. So, Menelaus, trusting Paris completely, left him to keep his wife company while he went on a diplomatic trip to Crete.

Helen had fallen in love with Paris from the minute he entered the palace, and Paris did nothing to resist her beauty. As soon as Menelaus had left, he suggested that they flee Sparta and go, as quickly as possible, to his home city of Troy, where they could live as man and wife.

When Menelaus came back, he found the couple had eloped. Attacking Troy by himself to get his wife back would have been impossible, but he remembered the promise that all the suitors had made to Helen's stepfather. He called on all the princes to join him in a campaign to destroy Troy, kill Paris and his entire family, and return Helen. He also asked others who owed him favors, including his brother Agamemnon, to help.

Most of the Greek chieftains responded favorably to his request, but there were two important holdouts. One was Odysseus, the king of Ithaca, a shrewd and sensible man who had no desire to leave his kingdom, his comfortable home, and his family to join an expedition that could bring him little profit and much trouble.

So, when Menelaus came to ask him to join his army, he pretended to be mad. He plowed his field himself, and threw salt instead of seeds in the earth. But Menelaus saw through the ruse. He seized Odysseus's little son and put him directly in the way of the plow. Odysseus, of course, turned the plow instantly, thus proving that he was sane. Reluctantly he had to agree to join the army of invaders.

The other holdout was the greatest warrior of them all—young Achilles. His mother, a sea nymph, knew that if he went to Troy he would die there. So she persuaded him to go to the court of another king, put on women's clothes, and hide among the maidens. When Menelaus could not find Achilles, he sent Odysseus, who was known as the wiliest of all the leaders, to look for him. Odysseus had been told at which court Achilles might be found, but could not discover him among the many young women. So, disguised as a peddler, he went to the women's quarters, bringing with him many fine garments and beautiful ornaments, along with some excellent weapons. All the women flocked around the clothing and jewelry, except one, who showed an interest only in the weapons. Obviously that person was Achilles, and Odysseus had no difficulty in persuading him that spending one's time in women's clothes, sewing and weaving, was not designed to bring honor to an ambitious young man. So, disregarding his mother's wishes, Achilles joined the Greek army.

While the many warriors were gathering, Agamemnon put together a great fleet. By the time everyone had arrived, more than a thousand ships were gathered at Aulis, ready to sail. But the north wind kept blowing day after day, making it impossible for the ships to move. The army began running out of food and water, and sickness started to make inroads in the camp. Agamemnon, who, as the most powerful of the kings, had been made the commander of the expedition, grew more and more desperate. Finally he called for a soothsayer, who told him the goddess Artemis was angry at him because he had slain one of her favorite wild animals, a hare. The only way to calm the storms and to insure a safe voyage to Troy was to sacrifice Agamemnon's young daughter, Iphigenia, on the altar of Artemis. To kill the beautiful and virtuous girl seemed terrible to many of the chiefs, but as the winds kept blowing and the conditions in the army camp got worse, Agamemnon decided that the sacrifice had to be made.

Agamemnon told himself and the other leaders that his only purpose in agreeing to the sacrifice was to uphold the honor of his country. But actually he was an ambitious man, and the idea of conquering Troy and carrying away all of the Trojan riches was more important to him than retrieving the unfaithful Helen.

So he sent word to his wife, Clytemnestra, telling her to bring Iphigenia to the camp. He had, he said, arranged a wonderful marriage for her. Her husband to be was the great hero, Achilles. Iphigenia and her mother came dressed for a wedding, delighted at the prospect. Instead, Agamemnon had some of his warriors seize the young girl and kill her on the altar of Artemis.

According to some other stories, Artemis never meant for Iphigenia to be killed. The message to Agamemnon had been garbled, probably by a jealous god or goddess. So, as the knife came close to the young girl's throat, Artemis whisked her away to a place where she would be safe. At any rate, neither her father nor her mother ever saw her again. Clytemnestra was never to forgive her husband for sacrificing her favorite daughter, and would eventually take terrible revenge on him (see Chapter 31).

As soon as the sacrifice had been completed, however, the north wind subsided, and a fleet of more than a thousand ships sailed out of the harbor toward Troy. Many of the heroes who had joined the Greek army knew that they would never see their homes or families again. Nowhere in the stories is there ever a clear indication of why so many brave and presumably reasonably intelligent men would be willing to sacrifice their lives for a cause as seemingly trivial as Helen's elopement with Paris.

The answer may lie with the gods. For not only did the Trojan War represent a struggle between the two most powerful nations in the world, but also between various factions of the gods of Olympus. Aphrodite, of course, was on the side of the Trojans. Hera and Athena were on the side of the Greeks. But why they took out their anger at Paris on so many innocent people is also never made clear. One wonders what had happened to those scales of justice Athena carried with her at all times.

At any rate, for nine years victory and defeat were always in the balance for both armies. Neither was able to gain a distinct advantage. The Greeks had brought many mighty warriors, but they were stationed on alien soil and, one may presume, supplying their army must have been a difficult problem. Also, there were constant battles among their leaders, who were proud and jealous men and who, during all those years of siege, had plenty of time to nurse the grudges they carried against each other.

On the other hand, the Trojans, led by their King Priam, were fighting from a fortified stronghold with high walls. Since the Greeks could never surround the city, Troy was easily resupplied from the fruitful countryside, and did not have the problems with famine and lack of clean water that plagued the Greeks. Also, the chief general of the Trojan army was Hector, a truly noble hero. He was honest and brave, strong and agile, and a faithful and loving husband and father. He must have had mixed feelings about the war, since from the beginning he knew that he was destined to die on the battlefield, and the city of Troy, which he loved, would be destroyed. His forebodings were reenforced by the prophecy of his sister Cassandra, who had been given the ability to foretell the future but the misfortune of never being believed. Still, Hector fought bravely, because his homeland had been attacked, and he felt that any attack against his people must be repelled.

The story the *Iliad* tells begins with the first serious crisis that arose among the Greeks. It was caused again by Agamemnon, who had been given a woman, Chryseis, as a prize of war. The Greeks, though they could not defeat Troy, had conquered other nearby cities and taken captives. Chryseis's father, a priest of Apollo, came to the Greek tents to beg for her release, but Agamemnon would not let her leave. The priest prayed to Apollo to avenge his honor and to bring his daughter back. Apollo heard him. From his chariot he shot fiery arrows into the Greek camp, which brought pestilence, and killed many of the soldiers.

Achilles, at the bidding of Hera, called a conference of all the Greek chieftains to try to find out why Apollo was angry. A man who had the gift of prophecy said Apollo was angry because of Chryseis. So Achilles insisted that Agamemnon return the priest's daughter immediately. But Agamemnon refused. "She was a prize of honor for me . . . and, if I give her up, I want another in her stead," he said.

The prize he picked out for himself was a beautiful young woman who belonged to Achilles. The girl was dragged away to Agamemnon's tent. Achilles, who easily could have killed Agamemnon's messengers, did not lift his sword against them because he knew that they were not at fault, but he swore vengeance against the man who had wronged him.

His mother, the sea nymph Thetis, who had not wanted him to go to war in the first place, was even angrier than her son. She turned to Zeus, who had once loved her, and asked him to make sure that the Greeks lost the war. Zeus, on the whole, considered the entire war rather stupid, and he liked King Priam and his family better than he did the impossible Agamemnon and his people. Besides, while the battles raged on earth, constant fights were disrupting the peace on Olympus. There were battles with Athena and Hera on one side and Aphrodite on the other. Apollo loved Hector, while Poseidon was on the side of the Greeks, who were great sailors. Zeus wanted to see all this discord end, one way or another, and he hated to deny the appeal of Thetis. So he thought of a way in which he could grant the sea nymph's request without irritating Hera, who would never have forgiven him for helping the Trojans.

He sent Thetis back to her son, to tell him to stay in his tent and not to participate in any battles for the time being. Then he arranged for Agamemnon to dream that if he attacked the next day his armies would be victorious. Actually, of course, Zeus knew that without the help of the mighty Achilles, the Greeks would lose, or at least they would suffer enough casualties to want to settle the whole matter in a way that would not destroy both armies.

Agamemnon, following the prophecy in his dream, attacked . . . and soon found out that he had made a mistake. The Trojan forces wreaked havoc on the Greek army. But the Trojans also lost many of their warriors. While the battle was on, Zeus arranged for Helen to appear on the wall of the city to watch the proceedings.

Many of the Trojan citizens looked at Helen; and thinking about what her beauty had caused, they said to each other, "Why are we allowing our husbands, sons, and brothers to be slaughtered for this worthless woman? If both Menelaus and Paris want her, why don't they fight for her in hand-to-hand combat?" They made this suggestion to the Greeks, who may also have been tired of the war, and it was agreed that Menelaus and Paris would fight for Helen. Whoever won would be allowed to keep her, and the war would be over. Zeus had tried to arrange a sensible solution, which should have pleased everybody. Except that Hera and Athena were not ready to be pleased.

The armies drew back, and Paris and Menelaus fought each other on the battlefield. Paris threw a spear at Menelaus, who caught it on his shield and hurled it back at Paris, whose tunic was torn, but who was not otherwise wounded. Then Menelaus drew his sword, but one of the gods caused it to break into two pieces. Now Menelaus was unarmed, but, stronger than Paris, he leaped on him, took hold of the crest of his helmet, and dragged him toward the Greek camp. This was something Aphrodite could not allow. After all, Paris was the one who had judged her to be the fairest of all goddesses. She made herself invisible, swooped down, and cut the strap on Paris's helmet. Then she hid Paris in a thick cloud and whisked him away, back to Troy.

Menelaus angrily searched through the ranks of the Trojan army to find his enemy, but Paris was not there. So Menelaus claimed that he had won the battle fairly. After all, having one's opponent vanish mysteriously in a cloud of smoke and not return to finish the fight could only be interpreted as voluntarily conceding. For once everyone agreed. Agamemnon said that if the Trojans were willing to return Helen, the Greek armies could go home. And the Trojans said that they would be delighted to give Menelaus back his unfaithful wife. For a few minutes it looked as if the war, so costly to both sides, was finally over.

However, everybody had planned without Hera and Athena. They wanted Troy destroyed. So they conspired to have Athena sweep down on the battlefield and induce a Trojan officer, Pandarus, to break the truce by shooting an arrow directly at Menelaus. He was wounded only slightly, but the Greeks considered the attack an act of treachery, and the battle was on again, fiercer and more bloody than before. The countryside echoed with the cries of the wounded and dying, and the ocean itself was red with the blood of Greeks and Trojans.

Even without Achilles, the Greeks were able to inflict many casualties on the Trojans, although they could not gain a decisive victory. Their two greatest heroes, except for Achilles, were Ajax and Diomedes. Diomedes and the Trojan prince Aeneas fought each other in hand-to-hand combat, and Aeneas was severely wounded. The Trojans, watching from their walls, thought he had been killed. What they did not know was that the mother of the prince was the goddess Aphrodite herself. She swooped down to save her son. Diomedes, who could not see her, hit with his sword in the direction of the escaping Aeneas, and inadvertently wounded Aphrodite in the hand. Goddess or not, Aphrodite could feel pain. She allowed Aeneas to fall to the ground and flew off, crying to Zeus to complain. He told her that love goddesses had no business getting involved in battles, and ordered her to stay away from wars from now on, but he graciously healed her cut. However, Apollo, who was very fond of Aphrodite (and still angry at the Greeks for stealing his priest's daughter), came down from Olympus and rescued Aeneas again. Aeneas was one of the few great fighters to survive the war; he lived a life of excitement and adventure, which was chronicled by the Roman poet Virgil.

Diomedes fought on, killing and wounding many more Trojans, until he came face to face with Hector. But, standing behind Hector was the god of war, Ares, a bloodstained and murderous figure. On seeing the god, Diomedes thought that the other citizens of Olympus had also turned their faces away from the Greeks, and called for his troops to fall back.

This really made Hera angry. She did not like Ares, even though he was her son, and she came to the side of Diomedes and told him not to fear Ares. "He may be a god," she said, "but he is also a bully and a coward. If you wound him, he will take himself off speedily." By now Athena had also entered the fight, and when Diomedes threw his spear at Ares, she made sure that it entered his body and hurt him a great deal.

Ares had brought suffering to millions of people over the ages, but when he was in pain himself, he did not bear his injuries like a hero. He bellowed at the top of his voice (frightening both the Greeks and the Trojans, so that they stopped their fighting for a few minutes) and fled back to Olympus. He too complained to Zeus. Zeus was thoroughly unsympathetic. He advised him, as he had Aphrodite, to stay away from battlefields if he did not wish to get hurt.

Hector had taken a brief rest from the fighting. But now, looking at the battlefield from the high Trojan walls, he felt that perhaps— in spite of his own instincts and his sister Cassandra's dire predictions —that one more brief battle might win the war for his countrymen.

He knew, however, that, no matter what the outcome of the war, he would die. So he sent for his wife, Andromache, and his baby son, Astyanax, to bid them good-bye. He loved them dearly, and they him. Indeed, this is one of the few truly happy marriages anywhere in Greek myth (which makes its tragic ending so truly heartbreaking).

Andromache begged her husband not to rejoin the battle. "You are everything to me," she told him. "Father and brother, as well as husband and lover. Do not make me a widow and your only child an orphan." But Hector had to refuse her. If there was any chance that his presence on the battlefield could put an end to the terrible fighting, he had to go, even if it meant his own death.

He rejoined the battle, and as soon as he appeared it looked as if the Greeks were once and for all really defeated. Even Agamemnon decided that perhaps the time had come to allow his army to return to their ships and sail home before his retreat was cut off by the rapidly advancing Trojans.

But again everyone had counted without Hera. She would never give up her hatred of the Trojans and would do everything she could to save the Greek army.

She knew that without some special kind of magic she had no influence on her husband at all. As a matter of fact, he seemed happiest when she was not anywhere near him. However, she also knew that Aphrodite had an ornament, a special belt (called a girdle in those days) that made her irresistible. So she borrowed the ornament and enchanted her husband so that he fell asleep in her arms.

At that point the battle again turned in favor of the Greeks. Ajax, one of the best Greek fighters, was even able to hurl the mighty Hector to the ground, but Hector's friend, Aeneas, lifted him up, and took him back to Troy. With Hector gone, the Greeks were able to advance so quickly that it looked for a little while as if they could storm the gates of Troy, and sack the city. But Zeus woke up, took one look at what was happening, and turned angrily to Hera.

"This is all your fault," he told her. "You deserve to be punished severely." Hera, among her many other faults, tended to blame somebody else whenever she got in trouble. She excused herself by telling her husband that the whole problem had been caused, not by her, but by Poseidon. But Zeus began helping the Trojans again, and the tide of battle once more turned against the Greeks.

Meanwhile Achilles sat in his tent, still nursing his hurt feelings over the insult Agamemnon had offered him. With him was his closest friend, Patroclus, whom he loved more than any other person on earth. Patroclus could no longer watch the rout of his countrymen. "If you don't want to help our friends, I must," he told Achilles. "I will borrow your armor, and join the battle. The Trojans will think that the greatest fighter of them all, Achilles, is back in the war and will hesitate in their attack. That will, perhaps, give us the advantage we need."

Achilles hesitantly allowed his friend to take the armor, but he himself still would not budge. "I cannot help a king who has dishonored me," he said.

For a while the trick worked. The Trojans thought that Achilles actually had come back to join the fight, and they retreated briefly. But Hector attacked Patroclus and killed him in a fair fight. He then stripped the magnificent armor Achilles had lent his friend from the dead body, and put it on. Again the Greeks were driven toward the shore, and it looked as if they might take refuge on their ships and return home in defeat.

As evening came, Achilles sat in his tent waiting for his friend to return. Instead, a messenger, weeping bitter tears, appeared. "Patroclus has been killed by Hector, and Hector has your armor," he told Achilles. The greatest hero of the Greeks seemed completely stunned by grief. He beat his chest, and cried so loudly that his friends feared he might take his own life. His mother, the sea nymph, came to comfort him, but to no avail. He swore that he would avenge Patroclus's death. "I am responsible because I allowed false pride to keep me in my tent," he cried. "Now I will kill Hector myself."

His mother reminded him of a prophecy that he would die very soon after Hector, but when she realized that she could not persuade him to stay out of the fight, she offered to get him the best weapons available. She would ask the god of the forge, Hephaestus, to make him a suit of armor that no sword made by mortal man would be able to penetrate.

In the morning, Achilles went to see Agamemnon and the other chieftains to tell them that he was rejoining the war, and that he personally would kill Hector. He swore that he would neither eat nor drink until he had avenged his friend.

The fiercest battle of the war now started. Led by Achilles, the Greeks advanced to the very gates of Troy. All the Trojan soldiers fled inside, but Hector remained, standing his ground against Achilles. He realized that this was a fight to the death. "If I kill you, I will give your body back to your friends, if you will do the same for me," he said, honorable as always.

But Achilles, in his bitter grief for Patroclus, was beyond such honorable compromises. As the hand-to-hand battle between the two greatest heroes of the war began, Hector quickly realized that he could not win. The magical suit of armor that Achilles wore could not be touched by sword or spear. Achilles aimed a spear at a spot in Hector's armor that he knew was weak. After all, the armor had once been his own. That opening was located near the throat, and he was able to pierce it with his weapon. As Hector lay dying on the ground, he asked with his last breath, "Please give my body back to my family for burial." But Achilles only swore at the dying man. He stripped the armor from the body, pierced the feet of the dead man, and fastened the thongs to the back of his chariot, letting the head trail. Then he spurred on his horses and dragged Hector's body around the walls of Troy, in full view of the dead hero's wife and parents, swearing that he would leave what was left for the dogs to devour.

On Olympus, Zeus was displeased. Hector had been his special favorite, and to dishonor his body was to dishonor the gods. He would not, however, interfere. Instead he sent a messenger to Priam, Hector's father, and let him know that if he went to Achilles tent with a wagon of gold and jewels to beg for his son's body, he would soften Achilles heart.

Priam, the courageous old king, went alone to the tent of his worst enemy. "Remember, Achilles, your own father," he said. "What happened to me could happen to him." Finally, Achilles was moved. He asked his servants to wash Hector's body, to place it in soft robes, and to return it to Priam.

So Hector received proper funeral ceremonies after all. But this was of little comfort to his despairing mother and wife. All of Troy wept for him, even Helen. Hector had been the only Trojan who had treated her with kindness, when everyone else blamed her for the disaster she had caused.

As had been prophesied, Achilles was killed shortly after he defeated Hector, but the war went on relentlessly, with casualties on both sides increasing.

The Greeks had now spent almost ten years away from their homes, and they were weary. The siege of Troy might be endless, unless some way could be found to penetrate the thick, high walls of the city. Paris had been killed by now, and certainly Helen might well have been returned to her husband. But almost everyone had forgotten the original cause of all the bloodshed. The war itself had become its own reason for being.

Finally Odysseus proposed a ruse that might allow a group of Greeks to get into Troy and to open the doors to the rest of the army. He had a craftsman build a huge wooden horse that was hollow inside. Then he persuaded Agamemnon to pretend to abandon the field of battle. Most of the warriors, with the exception of a few of the strongest and bravest, returned to their ships. The few selected men climbed inside the horse and waited.

The Trojans saw that the Greeks had left and, just as they were supposed to, became convinced that the terrible war was finally over. They joyfully opened their gates and went to inspect what was left of the Greek camp. There was very little. The winds whistled through the empty tents. And the Greeks seemed to be busy inside their ships, preparing them for a trip home. Then the Trojans saw with astonishment a gigantic horse that had been left behind. Near the horse, apparently in hiding, they found one Greek all by himself.

The man said his name was Sinon. Under threat of torture, with seeming hesitancy, he told the Trojans that the Greeks had planned to sacrifice him to the gods in return for a safe journey home, but that he had escaped. He said that the horse had been built as a special offering to Athena, and that whoever had it in his possession would find favor in that goddess's eyes.

The Trojans believed Sinon and took him and the horse into the city. They were warned, first by a priest, Laocoon, who urged them to destroy the wooden animal. "I fear the Greeks when they bear gifts," he said. Cassandra, the daughter of King Priam, agreed with him. But Athena, who was, of course, still on the side of the Greeks, and who was delighted with the scheme Odysseus had devised, caused two gigantic snakes to come out from her temple in

Troy and strangle the priest and his two sons. This, to the Trojans, seemed an infallible sign that Athena wanted the horse to be placed in front of her temple (as indeed she did, but not for the reasons the Trojans thought). They dragged the horse near the center of the city and had a huge victory celebration with the best food and wine available. Then almost everyone in the city went home to sleep.

In the dead of night, when all of Troy was quiet, Odysseus and the other Greeks hidden in the belly of the horse came out, threw open the gates of Troy, and let in the Greek army.

The Greeks had no difficulty in overcoming the surprised, half-drunk, and sleepy Trojans. They quickly set fire to the houses, and even tore the roof off the palace of Priam, lifting the tower from its foundation and toppling it over. Achilles' son killed the old king. By morning all the Trojan leaders, including the sons of King Priam, were dead. Only one had been saved. Aphrodite had spirited away her son Aeneas, but even she could not save his wife and children. They were separated from Aeneas and died in the confusion.

Aphrodite also decided to help Helen. She got her out of the city, took her to Menelaus, and so enhanced Helen's already devastating beauty that her husband took her back gladly. He sailed with her back to their home in Greece.

For the women and children of Troy worse was yet to come. All of them, including the old queen Hecuba and Hector's widow, Andromache, were carried off as slaves. Hector's little son was thrown from the high walls of Troy to his death. Just before the Greek soldiers killed him, they sacrificed, on the grave of Achilles, Hecuba's youngest daughter, Polyxena.

Then they carried all the other women and children away from their burning homes, never to return again. And that was the end of the Trojan War.

It had started in stupidity and false pride, and it ended with disaster for both sides. Of the Greek leaders, only Agamemnon, Menelaus, and Odysseus got back to their homes. All the others wandered from place to place or perished with their ships.

And Agamemnon might have wished that he had never left the Trojan shores, had he known what was in store for him.

PART SEVEN

After the Trojan War

Chapter 31

The House of Atreus:
Murder, Vengeance, and
Forgiveness

SOURCES: The story of the House of Atreus starts with Tantalus, the mortal who was honored by the gods and repaid them by serving them a meal of human flesh. He was forever subject to special punishment in Hades: Standing in spring water with delicious fruit hanging over his head, he was forever hungry and thirsty because he could never reach either drink or food.

His offspring were involved in a series of sins against the gods and each other. For instance, one of his grandsons seduced the wife of his brother. The brother killed the seducer's two little children, and served them to their father as a meal.

Agamemnon and Menelaus were the offspring of this murderous tribe. Actually, Menelaus seems, for some reason, to have escaped tragedy. He lost his wife, Helen, temporarily to Paris, but he apparently returned to Sparta and lived out his life in peace.

However, Agamemnon, his wife, and his children continued to live under the curse of the gods.

The sources for their story are ancient legends, which deal with the bloody murders among this family of vengeful and hate-ridden men and women. The Greek playwrights Sophocles and Aeschylus used those primitive stories to produce dramas that explored the human mind and soul. Aeschylus, especially, was fascinated by the tale of Agamemnon, his wife, Clytemnestra, his son, Orestes, and his daughter, Electra. He wrote a trilogy that turned a violent tragedy into an exploration of sin, justice, and, finally, forgiveness. It is his version of the story, basically, that is told here; but it is not the only version.

The story of Clytemnestra, Agamemnon, and Orestes has been an inspiration for artists throughout the centuries. Its powerful central tragedy has been used in painting, sculpture, plays based on the Greek tragedies, and even dance.

Most famous among the twentieth-century works are a drama by the great American playwright Eugene O'Neill called *Mourning Becomes Electra*, which transposes the action into nineteenth-century America, right after the Civil War, and a modern dance work choreographed by Martha Graham called *Clytemnestra*, which deals with the spiritual struggle of the queen and that of her son in highly emotional dance terms.

THE STORY: When Clytemnestra left Aulis after the Greek army had sailed for Troy, her heart was full of grief for her murdered daughter, Iphigenia, and fury at her cruel husband for having taken his young daughter's life. She blamed herself for having believed him when he told her that a marriage to Achilles had been arranged for her. After all, she had known her husband for a long time, and she might have suspected his treachery.

During the ten years that the Trojan War continued, her grief for her beautiful young daughter hardly lessened, and her hatred for her husband increased. She moved another man, Aegisthus, who for good reasons hated Agamemnon almost as much as she did, into the palace, and together they ruled as king and queen.

Besides Iphigenia, Clytemnestra had three other children, a son and two daughters. The oldest daughter, Electra, had loved her father and constantly reminded her mother that she was an unfaithful, immoral wife. She also sent her young brother, Orestes, away to live in another country because she was afraid that Clytemnestra's new lover would do him harm. Because her dislike and disapproval was so obvious, the royal couple punished her by making her live in poverty and disgrace. She was given a small hovel outside the palace gates as her home, dressed in rags, and allowed to do only the most menial work. Her sister, who did not make trouble for their mother, continued to live as a princess.

During the many years that Agamemnon was away at war, Clytemnestra would often stand by herself, gazing over the palace wall out on the barren plain where the castle stood. Often she prayed to the gods to have Agamemnon killed in battle. Even after the war was over, she still hoped that his ship would be caught in a storm and would sink, drowning everyone aboard.

But this did not happen. Finally, from her accustomed perch, she saw the victorious army, led by her hated husband, march toward the palace. She knew then and there that he must die.

The king was greeted with triumph and joy by the younger people of the city, but many of the old men remembered the death of the king's daughter and the curse that the gods had put on the whole family. Some of their greetings were mixed with anxiety. Obviously, trouble lay ahead, either for King Agamemnon or for his wife, whose seething anger was well known.

Agamemnon greeted Clytemnestra coldly. He had never really loved her and now he was carrying home a prize of war, the princess and prophetess Cassandra, daughter of Troy's King Priam. He ordered Clytemnestra to make sure that his beautiful young war prize was made to feel comfortable in the palace. Seeing her hated husband bring home a much younger rival, who might well be installed in her place, increased Clytemnestra's anger to burning fury, and she vowed that he would not spend one day in his home. She would make sure that he was dead by nightfall.

After Agamemnon entered the palace in a triumphant procession, Cassandra was briefly left outside the gates. Her prophetic powers told her that once she entered the castle she would die. As she was dragged into the palace, she cried out loudly, "No, this is a house God hates, where men are killed, and the floor is red with blood." Some of the old men listened and were frightened. But the younger people in the crowd just laughed at her and mocked her. It had been Cassandra's lifelong fate that she would always foretell the future correctly, but that nobody would believe her.

In the evening Clytemnestra ordered a victory feast with a great deal of wine served to her husband and the victorious generals, while the crowd outside waited for him to appear on a balcony to receive their praise. Suddenly, they heard a terrible cry. It was the king's voice. "I have been struck with a death blow," he screamed. Then they heard Cassandra cry out. Clytemnestra had murdered her as well as the king.

The crowd did not know what to do. Should they break into the palace and take control? But there was no time to make a decision. The door opened and the queen stood there covered with blood, a sword in her hand. She seemed completely calm and sure of herself. "My husband is dead, and I have killed him. My deed was just," she announced. "I punished the murderer of my youngest child." The crowd accepted the situation, and the queen and her lover, whom she now married, continued to rule for many years.

Electra remained in her miserable hut, living in poverty and waiting for the day when her brother, Orestes, would be old enough to avenge his father's murder. As Orestes grew into young manhood, he was never allowed to forget what Electra considered to be his duty. For him the situation was a terrible one. He knew what his mother had done. Yet for a son to kill his mother, for whatever reason, was an appalling sin in the sight of the gods. To try to resolve the awful puzzle, he went to Delphi to ask Apollo's oracle what he must do. Apollo told him that, as the only male relative, he must avenge his father's death to restore honor to his family. Orestes also knew, however, that such a murder could mean his own ruin.

Nonetheless, he started back to the home he had not seen since he was a very small child, accompanied by his cousin and friend, Pylades. The two boys had grown up together, and were very close.

Electra, who knew that the time had come for Orestes to return, spent every day at the tomb of her father, praying for her brother's safety. Orestes found her at the grave site and made himself known to her by showing her a special cloak she had made for him. She had dressed him in it when she sent him away.

Orestes let Electra know that the oracle of Apollo agreed with her: He must kill his mother, and, of course, her new husband, but that for him this was a heartbreaking task. He hardly knew Clytemnestra and had little reason to love her, but he shuddered at the very idea of lifting his sword against her.

The decision had been made for him, however, and the three young people planned how to accomplish the deed. They decided that Orestes and Pylades would go the palace claiming to be messengers sent to announce that Orestes had died in exile. This would be joyful news to Aegisthus and perhaps even to Clytemnestra, so they would be admitted with few questions. Once inside, they would use their weapons to accomplish their purpose. Surprise would be on their side, and they hoped to escape before the confused palace guards could arrest them.

Everything happened as they had expected, at least in the beginning. Orestes was able to slay Aegisthus, who was in the main hall. But Clytemnestra had come out to meet the messenger and heard her servant's screams when her husband was killed. She stood stock still, waiting for the young man whom she now knew to be her son. Then she ordered a servant to bring her a battle-ax. She had decided to fight for her life . . . even against Orestes.

He came running through the door, his sword dripping with blood, and she faced him. "Remember, I am your mother, who bore you and nursed you at her breast. To hurt me would be a terrible sin against nature and the gods," she said calmly. Orestes hesitated, but Pylades reminded him of the Delphi Oracle's command. Clytemnestra, seeing Orestes advance on her, sword drawn, knew that she could not dissuade him. Finally refusing to plead with him or to defend herself against him, she calmly went to her death.

When Orestes came out again, it was obvious that he had avenged his father, but he was not triumphant. He was numb with horror, sure that killing his stepfather had been just, but aware that only because of the Delphi Oracle had he been able to murder his mother.

Now some of the gods, who believed that the murder of a mother, for whatever reason, was an unforgivable sin, sent the Furies—a terrible group of flying females with beaks instead of noses, snakes instead of hair, and huge wings instead of arms—to pursue Orestes wherever he went, screeching and screaming into his ears that he was a hideous murderer.

For years he wandered over the earth, constantly pursued by the Furies, without a moment's rest or peace. When he finally returned to his own country, he was worn physically and emotionally from his suffering. Yet, he had come to the conclusion that, through his very misery, he might still win atonement, that perhaps no sin was severe enough never to deserve forgiveness. He traveled to Athens to plead his case before Athena, the goddess of justice.

The goddess listened to his plea, but was in doubt. And the Furies kept shouting that the kind of sin Orestes had committed *never* deserved forgiveness. But suddenly Apollo stood beside Orestes. "I ordered Orestes to commit that murder," he told Athena. "Therefore, I am responsible for his mother's death."

But Orestes would not accept the excuse. "You told me what to do, but I knew right from wrong, so I must take the responsibility for my own action," he said. "I have suffered for it, and I must be able to obtain atonement and forgiveness on my own without blaming anyone else, including Apollo."

It was this brave statement of responsibility that finally persuaded Athena. She acquitted Orestes, and with that acquittal, the curse that had for generations followed all members of the House of Atreus was lifted. Orestes went from Athens free from guilt and despair. Neither he nor any of his descendants would ever again be driven to murder, guilt, and evil by the irresistible power of the past. From now on, the remaining members of the House of Atreus and their children would be allowed to live in peace.

Chapter 32

The Adventures of Odysseus

SOURCES: The source of this story is Homer's *Odyssey*. Odysseus had appeared as a minor and often not very sympathetic character in some other myths. He was, of course, one of the main characters of Homer's *Iliad*, the leader who with his superior mind finally was able to devise a way to end that seemingly endless war.

In the *Iliad*, Odysseus is not a particularly sympathetic character. Everyone admires his cleverness, but few admire his honesty or charity. But in the *Odyssey*, Homer's attitude toward his principal character is different. Odysseus is intelligent and imaginative, but also loyal, brave, and, on occasion, kind. His physical strength is not what is most admirable about him; his moral and intellectual strength is what the reader is supposed to admire.

There are some experts who believe that the *Odyssey* may have been devised by a different poet than the one who created the *Iliad*, mainly because the values of the poet are different. However, it is equally possible to believe that the poet in different periods of his life looked on people and events through different eyes.

In many places in Greece, Odysseus is thought of as a real person, rather than a fictitious character. Since his travels presumably took him to almost every island and coastal harbor on the Aegean Sea, in most villages there is someone who insists that he or she knows a special place where Odysseus hid or camped out while on his journey back home. The cave of Odysseus is almost like the bed in which Washington slept. It's anywhere someone thinks it is.

THE STORY: The Trojan War was over, and all the gods and goddesses who had wished for the destruction of the city and the death of its rulers should have been satisfied. But many of them were not.

When the Greeks entered Troy, they had been intoxicated with their long-sought victory. They had celebrated with feasts, and had indiscriminately burned and pillaged the homes and temples of the city. They had not even respected the places that were considered sacred to specific gods, especially Athena and Poseidon. Athena was furious that her priestess, Cassandra, had been dragged from one of her temples, where she had sought refuge, and had been given as a slave to Agamemnon. Having satisfied their hostility toward the Trojans, the gods now turned their anger toward the Greeks, whom they considered lacking in respect and gratitude.

As the Greek ships left the safe harbor near Troy, Poseidon caused storms to blow and hurricanes to appear. Many of the ships sank, and all but a few of the Greek leaders and soldiers drowned.

We know that Agamemnon got home safely, but the gods' revenge (and that of his wife Clytemnestra) awaited him there. Menelaus got home safely to Sparta along with the beautiful Helen, who seems to have charmed the gods as well as her husband into forgetting her unwifely behavior. Another hero who would make his way home, but only after undergoing severe perils and trials, was Odysseus. He had gained Athena's affection, since he had not been involved in desecrating any temples, and had offered thanks to the gods for the long-sought victory and the chance of finally returning to his beloved wife and son.

Soon after leaving the coast of Troy, however, Odysseus's ship was caught in one of those terrible storms that Poseidon sent to destroy the Greeks. Odysseus was such an excellent navigator that his ship did not capsize. Instead, it landed in a sandy harbor on an island he had never seen before.

The island belonged to the Lotus Eaters, a group of people who cultivated a flower that they gave to travelers for refreshment. Once travelers had eaten the flower, they lost all memory of their past life and never wanted to leave the island again.

Odysseus quickly recognized what was happening when three

of his sailors who had been most eager to get home ate some of the food that was offered and refused to budge. They had to be dragged back to the ship by force, and Odysseus ordered the rest of his crew not to touch any of the food they were given, no matter how hungry they might be.

At the next island on which they landed, an even worse fate awaited them. Since there was not enough food and fresh water left on the ship, Odysseus and twelve of his men decided to go exploring to see if they could find a river or a spring and some wild game or fruit to replenish their supplies. What they did not know was that the island belonged to the Cyclops Polyphemus. Of all the Cyclops that Zeus had spared after his war with his father, Polyphemus was the most fearsome. He was as large as the highest oak tree, with arms and legs as thick as boulders. And, like all his brothers, he had one huge, red eye in the middle of his forehead. His favorite food was human flesh, and the occasional traveler who accidentally stumbled on his island was invariably eaten alive.

When he returned to his cave that night, with his one eye, Polyphemus noticed the small group of men who had assembled there and had eaten some of his food. He was delighted to see them. Here was the breakfast, lunch, and dinner he liked best. And because he had rolled a huge stone in front of the entrance Odysseus and his companions were trapped.

The Cyclops quickly snatched up two of the men and swallowed them whole. Then he stretched himself out on his huge bed and went to sleep. Odysseus wanted to kill the Cyclops, but he knew this was impractical. He and his men would then be trapped in the cave. So the little group waited until morning, saw two more of their number devoured, and then were left in the locked cave while the Cyclops went out to tend his flocks. Then it was time to plot an escape. The swords that Odysseus and his companions carried were much too small to do the giant any harm. They hardly could have inflicted the equivalent of needle pricks on him.

But he and his men used those swords to shape one end of a huge staff of olive wood into a spear with a sharp point. That night, after drugging the Cyclops with wine, they rolled the pointed end of the spear to the fire, which kept the cave warm, and heated it until it glowed red-hot. With one mighty push they aimed the hot, sharp instrument directly at the Cyclops's one eye and blinded him. Then they hid among the herd of sheep.

The giant leapt up and screamed with pain and rage; but he was blind and could not find his enemies. He used his huge hands to feel all the walls of the cave, but all he touched was sheep wool. Assuming then that his would-be victims had somehow managed to escape the cave, he rolled away the heavy stone (something that the humans who were hiding never could have accomplished) and started feeling the earth outside the entrance. While he was busy, Odysseus told his companions to hold on to the bellies of the sheep, and to drive them out of the cave and back to where the boat was anchored. The Cyclops could feel that his sheep were leaving, and he examined their backs because it occurred to him that the men might be clinging to them. But it never occurred to him to also search their bellies.

Odysseus and his friends got back to their boat, and took along some of the sheep for food. Athena made sure that a friendly wind was blowing, and they sailed away from the island, hoping never to see it or anything like it again. But the Cyclops had the last word. He prayed to Poseidon that all sorts of problems should plague Odysseus on his way home, and that prayer was answered.

From the island of the Cyclops, Odysseus and his crew traveled to a friendlier place: the Country of the Winds, ruled by King Aeolus, who was a special favorite of Zeus. Zeus had given the king power over the four winds, and after hearing the sad tale of the Greeks' long absence from home, the king decided to help the sailors reach Ithaca safely. He gave Odysseus a sack, tightly closed, containing the strongest winds. As long as no one opened it, there would be no more storms, and the journey home would go smoothly.

But some of the ship's crew did not believe the story. They thought that their captain had been given a sack full of gold, and that he was simply greedy in refusing to share it with his crew. So at a time when Ithaca was in sight, they opened the sack, and all the winds rushed out, blowing up a fierce hurricane that almost capsized the ship. It took days for the tempest to quiet down, and when it did, they were again on the island ruled by Aeolus, who refused to give them further help.

Discouraged, they set forth and eventually came to the land of the witch Circe, a beautiful but evil woman, who turned any man who approached her into an animal. The worst part of the enchantment was that the human being who became a beast always remembered what he had been before. He knew that he had been human, but that now he was completely under the power of the witch.

Odysseus sent a small exploring party onto the island. The men met Circe and were delighted by her beauty and her offer of hospitality. Of course, as soon as she had them safely in her house, she turned them all into swine. Then she mocked them, and gave them acorns to eat.

When his men did not return, Odysseus went after them; but Athena, who worried about what might happen, sent Hermes to warn him, and to give him a magical herb that would ward off Circe's spell. When Circe met Odysseus, she was all friendliness and kindness, and invited him to her home for a spectacular feast. Of course, as soon as he entered the door, she tried to cast her spell. But Odysseus was fortified with Hermes' magical herbs, and, for the first time, the spell did not work.

Odysseus drew his sword and threatened to kill her if she did not use her magic to return all those she had enchanted back into human beings. She did so reluctantly. But Circe was so amazed at Odysseus, the only man who had been able to resist her spell, that she fell in love with him. And since he and his crew were tired and sick, she persuaded them to stay with her for a year. When Odysseus saw that he and his crew had recovered their health and strength, he told her that they must leave. By now she had grown so fond of all her guests that she decided to use her magical powers *for* rather than *against* them. She told them what they must do next in order to assure a safe passage home.

They must sail their ship to a harbor on the shore of Hades, where they would have to find the ghost of an ancient prophet. He would tell them what other dangers awaited them and how they might avoid getting caught. The Greeks did what they were told, and found the entrance to the terrible underworld after many months. Circe had told them that they must sacrifice their sheep (the ones they had taken from the island of the Cyclops) because the ghosts who lived in Hades loved to drink blood, and would come out to greet them when the sacrifice was made.

What Circe had predicted came true. The ancient prophet met them and told them that whatever else happened there was one danger they must avoid at all costs: They must not injure the golden oxen of the sun, whom they were bound to meet. Any man who harmed them was doomed. The prophet also predicted that Odysseus himself would definitely reach his home, although many of his men would not, and that a great deal of trouble awaited him there.

From Circe, the Greeks had also learned that they would be passing the island of the Sirens, beautiful maidens who sat on rocks overlooking the ocean and sang wonderful songs that made men lose their reason. Countless ships had run into those rocks when sailors forgot to navigate properly, and hundreds of skeletons littered the beach near the Sirens' rocks. Odysseus knew exactly what to do: He insisted that all of his crew members put wax in their ears so that they would not hear the Sirens' songs. But he wanted to know what it was that so distracted men, so he had himself lashed to the main mast of the ship and ordered his men to pass the rocks by, no matter what he might order when he was under the enchantment of the music.

The Sirens' song was indeed beautiful, but the words were even more seductive than the melody. The Sirens promised that they knew all things, and that they could give any man who came to them knowledge not even possessed by the gods. This was, of course, why so many had been tempted to their deaths. Odysseus, too, was enchanted and begged his men to land their ship on the beach. But they had wax in their ears and could not hear him, so they passed this danger by safely.

The next peril that awaited them was the passage between huge cliffs called Scylla and a whirlpool, Charybdis. One created a vortex that drew ships into the depth of the water. The other drew ships to crash on its rocks and devoured sailors. Odysseus, with the help of Athena, was able to get them through the passage, but six of his crew members lost their lives.

Their next stopping place was the land of the sun, where the beautiful golden oxen roamed. The men were very hungry by that time and decided that the warning of the ancient prophet had probably been just so much nonsense. So while Odysseus was away, they killed several of the sacred oxen. The vengeance of the gods was swift. As soon as the men got back on their ship, a thunderbolt hit it, and they were all killed except Odysseus, who was able to cling to the keel of the ship and ride out the storm. He drifted on for days, until he finally washed up on the island of a nymph, Calypso.

Calypso fell in love with him and planned never to let him go. He had no ship, so he could not get away. For seven years he stood on the shore of the lovely island, looking in what he thought might be the direction of Ithaca, wracked by homesickness and longing for the wife and son he had left so long ago. Poseidon was delighted. He had never meant for Odysseus to get home, but Athena decided that her favorite should get his wish. So when Poseidon was busy somewhere else, she went to Zeus and requested that he order Calypso to let Odysseus go and to help him build a vessel that could carry him to Ithaca.

Zeus sent Hermes to let Calypso know that she must allow her guest to get on with his journey. She was even persuaded to order her servants to help him build a raft, which, with luck, would carry him to his homeland.

But Athena did more than just free Odysseus. There was a great deal of trouble in his castle, just as the old prophet had predicted. Most of the inhabitants of the country, after almost twenty years, did not think that their king was ever coming home. Odysseus's wife, Penelope, was not only very beautiful, but also the queen of a fine, rich country, and so hundreds of suitors had gathered at her palace to try to persuade her to marry one of them and make the chosen one king. Penelope loved only Odysseus and refused the suitors, who became more and more importunate. They did not go home after having been refused, but stayed on, eating and drinking merrily every evening, destroying the beautiful furniture of the castle with their drunken brawls.

They also threatened her son, Telemachus, a strong, brave, and discreet young man, who much resembled his father. Penelope took these threats seriously, and with the help of Athena, who liked Telemachus as much as she did Odysseus, had the young man spirited away to Sparta, where he lived in the house of Menelaus. Athena assured him that she would bring him back to Ithaca when his father had returned, and when his presence might be needed.

Meanwhile, Penelope held off the impatient suitors by telling them that she could not possibly even think of marrying anyone until she had completed a sacred duty, the weaving of a special cloak that was to be a shroud for the body of Odysseus's father. Only she made sure that she never finished the task. Every day she wove and spun, and every night she undid what she had accomplished during the day. However, as the days and months went by, the suitors became increasingly rude. And when one of the servants betrayed her and told the men that she had fooled them, they insisted that she make up her mind quickly, or they would *force* her to marry one of them.

While his wife was trying to devise new ways to get all those impossible suitors out of her house, Odysseus had landed the raft, which he had navigated all by himself, on the shores of the land of the Phoenicians. They turned out to be friendly and helpful.

The king was moved to tears by Odysseus's tale of courage and endurance, and gave him a ship manned by some of his best sailors to take him—finally—back to Ithaca. Athena, who had been watching her favorite's movements, decided that the time had come for her to get Telemachus back to his home, too. Considering the situation in Ithaca, Odysseus would need all the help he could get.

Because the goddess knew that if Odysseus was recognized by one of the suitors, he would probably be killed, she advised him, as he set foot on Ithaca, to dress like an old beggar. As such, his first night at home was spent not in the palace, but in the hut (or sometimes said, a cave) of his swineherd Eumaeus, who had always been honest and loyal, but who did not suspect that the old-looking man in the beggarly clothes was his long-lost master.

Athena then guided Telemachus to the same hut or cave. The young man had been a baby when his father left for war twenty years before. But he was generous and charitable, and he smiled at the old beggar and told him that he was glad the swineherd had made the stranger comfortable. Then when Eumaeus was gone, Athena, in a flash, turned Odysseus back into his royal self. His rags vanished, and he stood with his purple cloak and shining armor before his son. "I am your father," he said, "and I am delighted and proud to see what a fine and generous young man you have become."

The two men wept tears of joy and embraced each other. They spent much of the night in conversation, recounting what had happened in the past years. Then they had to decide what to do about the situation at the palace. There were only the two of them against that horde of suitors, who certainly were not going to give up and leave in peace. They would have to be thrown out of the palace or killed.

Both men decided that they should go to the palace, Odysseus, of course, keeping his disguise. Then, when all the suitors were sleeping off the wine they drank every night, father and son would hide all their weapons, leaving only enough for the two of them in a place where they could easily reach them.

As both men entered the palace, an old dog lying near a fire lifted his head and pricked up his ears. Of all those whom Odysseus had known, his dog was the only being who recognized him immediately. He wagged his tail and tried to drag himself across the floor to lie at his master's feet, but he was too old and sick to move. Odysseus brushed away a tear. He wanted to go to his old pet, but he was afraid that if he did the others might realize who he was, so he turned away. The dog let out what sounded like a deep sigh, and died. He had apparently only lived for the past twenty years to await his master's homecoming.

In the hall the suitors were gulping down another rich meal and drinking a great deal more of their hostess's fine wine than was good for them. They mocked the old beggar and laughed at his ragged clothing. But Penelope would not allow anyone in her home to be insulted by her other guests. She sent for him and asked him how he got to Ithaca, and why he had come. He told her that he had met her husband in Troy many years before, and that he had spoken so well of his wife that he had been sure he would receive kind hospitality at her house. Penelope asked many questions about Odysseus, and wept bitter tears, telling the beggar that she had missed her husband terribly.

She also asked one of her oldest and most trusted servants to help take care of her guest, and suddenly Odysseus was again with someone who could recognize him. The servant had been his nurse when he was a very young boy. He had hurt his foot in a hunting accident, and as she removed his sandals, she recognized the scar. But Odysseus signaled to her not to let anyone else know his identity. And when it was time to sleep, he lay down on the floor near the banquet hall; there he planned how he and his son could overcome all those suitors when they woke up in the morning.

Penelope, who was still trying to avoid having to marry one of the suitors, had come up with a scheme that he decided would be of use to him. Odysseus had owned a bow and a set of arrows that no one else had been able to use because the bowstring was so tight it took enormous skill and strength to pull it back. Now Penelope proposed that the suitors use this in a shooting contest. She would hang ten rings from the ceiling, and would marry the first man who could use the bow to shoot an arrow through all the rings.

In the morning, the men handed the bow around, but not one suitor could budge the tightly strung weapon. Then the old beggar in the corner said, "Since every man in this room has been asked to compete, by right I also should have a chance." All the suitors just laughed. If they were not strong enough to handle the weapon, how could a poor old man possibly beat them in the contest? But Telemachus knew that once his father had the bow, he could shoot the suitors one by one. Their weapons were hidden, and they would not be able to defend themselves. So he stood behind his father and handed him one arrow, which Odysseus shot through the ten rings without the slightest difficulty. The second arrow that his son gave him he shot through the heart of the most obnoxious of the suitors, and then he aimed his arrows, one after another, at the other unwelcome guests in his house. When several of them tried to attack him with their bare hands, Telemachus quickly reached for a sword he had hidden nearby, and within a short time all the drunken, rowdy fellows who had made the household miserable for years were dead. Odysseus spared only one: a young man who was a poet and a singer as well as a warrior, and who begged for his life. Like all Greeks, Odysseus had great respect for artists, and he knew also that the gods favored men who were accomplished in poetry and music. So he told the man to start using his talents in more acceptable ways, and to mend his manners. And then he let him go.

Finally he was able to tell Penelope that he was her husband, returned after twenty years of war and travel. At first she did not believe him. He had changed so much, from youth to middle age. But his old nurse pointed to the scar on his foot, and Telemachus let his mother know that Athena had told him that this man was his father. She looked deeply into his eyes and saw that after all these years he was, after all, still the man she had married. She cried tears of joy, and he kissed and embraced her and told her how much her love and loyalty had meant to him. "There are few men in this universe who can count on a woman the way I could count on you," he told her.

The people of Ithaca were also delighted to have their king back, and Odysseus, Penelope, and Telemachus were able to rule the realm with peace and happiness for all. Odysseus had seen enough of strife and suffering never to want another war. He was also an expert diplomat, so that, even without fighting, his country became one of the most prosperous in the world.

The gods, who had spent the past twenty years warring among themselves over the humans who fought the Trojan War, also reconciled. Athena was delighted that Odysseus was home and had acquitted her faith in him. Even Poseidon had to agree that he had proved to be an excellent sailor. And Hera and Aphrodite decided to reconcile. Zeus, too, was pleased that for once it looked as if the people on earth could live in peace and prosperity, and that the quarrels among his godly family were apparently settled—at least for the time being.

BIBLIOGRAPHY

Bulfinch, Thomas. *Bulfinch's Mythology*. New York: Avanel Books, 1978.

Frazer, Sir James. *The New Golden Bough* (abridged). New York: New American Library, 1964.

Graves, Robert. *The Greek Myths*. New York: Penguin Books, 1960.

Hadas, Moses, ed. *Greek Drama*. New York: Bantam Books, 1977.

Hamilton, Edith. *Mythology*. New York: New American Library, 1942.

Kerenyi, C. *Myth and Man: The Heroes of the Greeks*. Northampton, England: Thames and Hudson, 1974.

Oates, Whitney J., and Eugene O'Neill, Jr. *The Complete Greek Drama*. New York: Random House, 1938.

Shelley, Percy Bysshe. *Prometheus Unbound*. In *The Complete Poetical Works of Percy Bysshe Shelley*. New York: Oxford University Press, 1974.

Wood, Michael. *In Search of the Trojan War*. New York: Facts on File, 1985.

INDEX